The Executioner exploded in the other direction, drawing his .45

"Nice trick," Augustyn called out.

Bolan heard him reload his half-depleted handgun. The Executioner remained silent, waiting for his opponent to reveal himself. Augustyn's chatter was meant to distract Bolan, covering noises. The way the apartment was laid out, with soundproofed walls, there was no certain way to locate Augustyn by sound, though the noise of reloading or acquiring new weapons could be heard.

Bolan cursed himself for not taking down Eugene in a quieter manner, but the business manager was fit and brawny enough to turn a struggle into an extended wrestling match had he taken any other approach. Lethal force would have left Bolan behind the curve in figuring out what Augustyn had just been hired to do. Considering Eugene's voiced disgust, it had to be bad, and he assumed a lot of people would die.

Bolan had just declared

D1359001

MACK BOLAN ®
The Executioner

The Don Pendleton's
Executioner®
OUTBACK ASSAULT

A GOLD EAGLE BOOK FROM
W🦅RLDWIDE®

TORONTO • NEW YORK • LONDON
AMSTERDAM • PARIS • SYDNEY • HAMBURG
STOCKHOLM • ATHENS • TOKYO • MILAN
MADRID • WARSAW • BUDAPEST • AUCKLAND

First edition June 2008

ISBN-13: 978-0-373-64355-4
ISBN-10:   0-373-64355-1

Special thanks and acknowledgment to
Doug Wojtowicz for his contribution to this work.

OUTBACK ASSAULT

Cruelty in war buyeth conquest at the dearest price.
—Sir Philip Sidney
1554–1586

My enemies are those who violate the places
ordinary people hold sacred. For their careless rush
to quench their burning greed, I will exact a price
that will not be placid or kind.
—Mack Bolan

THE
MACK BOLAN

LEGEND

Nothing less than a war could have fashioned the destiny of the man called Mack Bolan. Bolan earned the Executioner title in the jungle hell of Vietnam.

But this soldier also wore another name—Sergeant Mercy. He was so tagged because of the compassion he showed to wounded comrades-in-arms and Vietnamese civilians.

Mack Bolan's second tour of duty ended prematurely when he was given emergency leave to return home and bury his family, victims of the Mob. Then he declared a one-man war against the Mafia.

He confronted the Families head-on from coast to coast, and soon a hope of victory began to appear. But Bolan had broken society's every rule. That same society started gunning for this elusive warrior—to no avail.

So Bolan was offered amnesty to work within the system against terrorism. This time, as an employee of Uncle Sam, Bolan became Colonel John Phoenix. With a command center at Stony Man Farm in Virginia, he and his new allies—Able Team and Phoenix Force—waged relentless war on a new adversary: the KGB.

But when his one true love, April Rose, died at the hands of the Soviet terror machine, Bolan severed all ties with Establishment authority.

Now, after a lengthy lone-wolf struggle and much soul-searching, the Executioner has agreed to enter an "arm's-length" alliance with his government once more, reserving the right to pursue personal missions in his Everlasting War.

Prologue

Arana Wangara was jerked awake by the distant roar of guns cracking in the night. Before she could cry out in dismay, a weathered old hand covered her mouth.

"They will not see us, child," came a rough whisper. "Sorry, Arana. I keep forgetting you're not a child."

Grandfather Wangara's voice soothed her, but she wasn't certain that the darkness was cover enough in the outback. For the first time in her eighteen years, she believed that she could die, and the realization chilled her to the bone.

"It's all right," she whispered, lying. Her brown eyes were wide and staring to where she could see distant flickers.

The starlit sky, spread out like broken glass on blue velvet, was obscured by the roof of the simple mud hut they'd been sleeping in. Through the doorway, the rolling, dusty terrain looked like dark, frozen waves under the glimmering night sky. With no pollution or electric lights for hundreds of miles, it was a serene, beautiful view that belied the cacophony rumbling in the distance. In the darkness, two Aboriginal tribesmen, their skins as dark as coal, were invisible. Dark-toned clothing helped conceal them under the shadows of their quickly erected hut.

Grandfather had been right to take her and leave their tiny cabin to sleep in a hidden lean-to on the edge of their property, she realized. Ever since the troubles had begun, they'd felt no safety. The sheriff was either too scared or too well bribed to bother to take an interest in the affairs of the Chinese businessmen and their real-estate "transactions" with the Aboriginal Tribal Council.

Arana wrinkled her nose, brow furrowing in frustration. She knew that those transactions had begun to include a bullet in the head and a short trip to the bottom of a shallow grave. The Chinese and their local assistants were nothing more than a pack of savages who were only interested in finding a nice, secluded spot twenty kilometers from the great Uluru mound, the mystical gateway to the Dreamtime.

Arana didn't know about the truth of the Dreamtime, but Grandfather Wangara's wisdom seemed to come from sources far beyond those of normal men.

"We are far from our old doorstep, and we have night's protection," her grandfather told her. "It would take them hours to find us."

Her grandfather said that the Chinese would not notice them, and Arana finally felt calm until a powerful crack split the night, a mushroom of fire rising from where their home had once been. Her stomach twisted as the fireball hung lazily, illuminating the gunmen surrounding the house. The building glowed from within.

Arana closed her eyes to the sight, not wanting to see

her home burned to the ground. Her grandfather's hand rested on her shoulder, his weathered face highlighted by the glow of the inferno. She looked up and saw the tears trickle over his cheeks, but his face remained an impassive mask. His brown eyes were unfocused, a sign that he was in touch with the Dreamtime.

Arana pursed her lips and looked back. The men got into their jeeps after their act of arson, not even bothering to pick up the gasoline cans that they'd used to soak the walls. When the law was too timid to poke its nose in, what need was there to hide the evidence? Somewhere, powerful forces were at work to accommodate the Chinese.

All it meant to her was that she and her grandfather had to leave, to run away from the only home she'd ever known. It filled her with anger.

"There will come a man," the old man whispered. "A crusader who has faced these lowly criminals before. And when he arrives, he will bring death with him, to cleanse the outback."

Arana looked at him.

"You will meet him in Darwin. And you will know him for his eyes are as cold as a winter sky," her grandfather said.

"Darwin? We don't have enough money to go there, and even if we did, they would follow us," Arana explained, confused.

"I shall not be making the journey with you. I will remain here. The Dreamtime will protect me," Grandfather told her. "You will go on your own. And though they shall try to interfere with your journey, you will be too clever for them. But remember, your skill will expire the moment you need it most, though luck and the crusader will catch you before you fall."

Arana swallowed hard.

Grandfather Wangara pressed a roll of money into her palm. "Go swiftly, child. Time is of the essence, and the crusader is turning his eyes to our plight even as we speak."

Arana nodded. She grabbed her backpack and took off, running across the desert. It was twenty miles to the nearest town, and there she'd catch the bus to Alice Springs. From there, it'd be an even longer ride to Darwin.

Her grandfather, though, was rarely wrong.

On a wing, a prayer, and a healthy slice of blind faith, Arana raced toward town, staying to gullies and ruts in the sand. Dawn was seven hours away, but if she hurried, she'd be at the bus stop shortly after sunrise.

The penthouse apartment was palatial in scope. Twenty-five stories above the streets of Hong Kong, the multi-tiered dwelling would have qualified as a mansion in any other city in the world. The terrace included an expanse of lawn dotted with shade trees, as well as a swimming pool surrounded by polished black marble tile. The three-story dwelling had a large patio that looked out over Victoria Harbour. It was so high that in the shadow of night, the lights of the floating shantytown in the bay looked like a simple extension of Hong Kong's vibrant streets.

The penthouse was the home of Wade Augustyn, a man considered by the outside world to be a polite, very private gentleman. Augustyn was known as a moderately wealthy philanthropist on the Hong Kong scene, but whispered back-street rumors had brought him to the attention of Mack Bolan. Bolstered by intelligence from Stony Man Farm, Bolan had determined that Augustyn was in the employ of the triads and the Chinese SAD, the Communist nation's premier security organization.

Augustyn was a "cleaner." He solved problems for his

criminal and government cohorts one bullet at a time, usually from a comfortable distance. The death trail Bolan was tracking was long and twisted, especially when Augustyn had begun to operate not only in the criminal sphere, but also interfered with U.S. intelligence operations in the Orient. Augustyn's alleged hit list included honest lawmen and operatives fighting for the security of the West against Beijing's less than honorable pursuits.

The final nail that had marked Augustyn's coffin was the execution of an American agent who was working behind the scenes trying to eliminate sensitive data that had been seized aboard a captured U.S. Navy spy plane. The agent's dying actions had been two button presses, one to capture Augustyn's face, the other to launch a desperate e-mail. With that action, Augustyn had been added to Stony Man Farm's watch list.

Agent Lissa Reynolds's final cell-phone digital image had been transmitted to the Farm. Reynolds had once been part of the Farm's blacksuit operation, one of the few women tough and qualified enough to hang with the commandos and special agents who made up Stony Man's security and training force. Bolan had met Reynolds only once, and she'd impressed him with her professionalism. That professionalism and unyielding determination had been cut off mercilessly.

Bolan looked at the rifle on the rooftop next to him. The Remington 700 was a nondescript hunting rifle, chambered for 7 mm Remington Magnum. Given the chance, the Executioner preferred a clean, antiseptic kill, and the high-powered hunting rifle would provide that in spades. Across the street from Augustyn's penthouse, he was in a perfect position to pull the trigger on the man made wealthy by the blood of good people.

Unfortunately, after half a day's stakeout, Bolan had only learned that the man was out of town, returning that night. In the meantime, the other distant reaching tool that Bolan had at his disposal, a long-range directional microphone, had picked up phone data. He called the Farm to see who was trying to get in touch with the assassin, but Augustyn's penthouse was electronically secured. Except for the faint warble of his phone, Bolan's microphone could pick up nothing thanks to a white noise generator. Even Aaron "The Bear" Kurtzman and his cybercrew were incapable of breaking through Augustyn's encrypted telephone lines, meaning that the wealthy killer had put as much work into securing his home as he did making it look luxurious.

"He just landed at the airport, Striker," Kurtzman advised. "His driver won't take long to get him home, and we haven't made a dent in his system. By the time he gets there, he'll know we've been trying to intrude because we tripped over some truly amazing black ice."

Bolan knew enough of hacker-speak to know that "black ice" was a form of electronic security. For the cybercrew to be caught off guard by such measures was more circumstantial evidence that Wade Augustyn was someone with a lot to hide. It could be the industrial secrets of a less than honest businessman, but combined with Reynolds's last photograph, in the court of Bolan's opinion, it was more than enough to warrant a hard probe.

Bolan abandoned the mike and the rifle. Both had been picked up locally, and had been sanitized of fingerprints and DNA residue, in case the SAD discovered them. They'd be considered just two more pieces of black market equipment smuggled into China by foreign devils like the Yakuza or the Americans. As he made his way across the street, concealed on his person were a Chinese-made Norinco, a copy of the venerable Colt .45, and a silenced .32-caliber Walther PPK. It wasn't his usual load in the field, but it was what was available.

The Executioner rode two elevators to reach Augustyn's residence. The elevators took him as far as the floor beneath Augustyn's. The top levels were accessible only via a private car that Bolan couldn't get into without a security code. Kurtzman tried to open the system, but electronic countermeasures stonewalled the computer wizard. With the assassin's homecoming only minutes away, Bolan would have to make do with more primitive means. As soon as the car reached the twenty-fourth floor, he stood on a side rail, punched through the access hatch and clambered on top. He tugged on thick leather gloves and climbed the ropes one level.

There were no doors, but there was a ventilation duct access. Bolan scanned it with a flashlight and picked up the presence of pressure sensors on the grating. He fished a 25,000-volt stun gun from his breast pocket and pressed the spikelike leads to the edge of the grating. He tapped the firing stud for two seconds, then flicked on the stun gun's safety. It was a trick that Stony Man's Hermann "Gadgets" Schwarz had taught him—a means of temporarily disabling an electronic sensor. The scorch marks it left behind were messy and provided telltale signs of the intrusion, but the Executioner didn't intend to hang around Hong Kong long enough for that to matter.

Bolan removed the grating and entered the ventilation system, crawling to the first opening. A solid kick smashed the grate out, allowing him to slither into Augustyn's penthouse suite. He'd only needed enough stealth to cross the street without drawing police attention. Now, hundreds of feet above street level in a home that was shielded by white noise generators and soundproofed walls and floors, the Executioner had a wide-open killing ground safe from Chinese interference, either from above or below the law. At the most, he figured he'd have to deal with Augustyn's chauffeur, who would either have bodyguard training or be a professional killer in his own right.

Following the floor plans that Kurtzman had provided on the building, he moved to where the private elevator would be. It was secured behind a pair of ornate oak doors that, when opened, proved to be extremely heavy. Bolan could feel the weight of a sheet of armor plate sandwiched between the layers of thick, decorative wood.

The first floor had been tastefully decorated. Hardwood floors gleamed with no sign of heel scuffs marring their beauty even where Bolan had crossed them. He left the doors open, drew the .45 and let it hang low at his side while he searched the apartment. Minimal lighting made the place navigable.

A burst of static suddenly sounded over Bolan's earphone. He flicked off the safety on his Norinco. He knew that Kurtzman had tried to get through to him. There had to have been only a narrow band through which communications could pierce the bubble of security that Augustyn had installed. Since Bolan was operating on a satellite signal, and his cell phone wasn't coded for the encryption static that engulfed the apartment, he was unable to make out Kurtzman's message.

It didn't matter. The attempt to break through produced enough noise to alert the Executioner that Augustyn had arrived. Bolan returned to the huge doors and closed them. The latch snapped shut with an audible click and he turned. He put himself in the mentality of a world-traveling businessman. He spotted a space atop an intricately carved table where Augustyn would probably empty his pockets and with just a single step and a press of a button, access the messages left for him when he was out.

The hired assassin had a layer of anonymity between himself and his employers. As a matter of survival for Augustyn, he'd likely only take communications in his very secure home, not on the road with a cell phone. The potential to be traced by cellular signal was too great to secure Augustyn's privacy.

Bolan took a step toward the answering machine and studied the sleek, disklike device. It had to have been cutting-edge technology either straight from Tokyo, or knocked-off in a Hong Kong back-alley electronics lab. He pushed the button and the digital player cycled through its memory, bringing up the three priority messages that had drawn Kurtzman's attention.

"We need you. Tickets have been arranged for you to travel to Darwin. We'll have a contact brief you on the cleanup," the first message announced. The other two were identical to the first, no change in urgency, and had been spaced a day apart.

Nonpriority messages began to play on the sleek machine, but Bolan killed the playback. The machine requested to know if he wanted to retain the trio of messages as priority, and Bolan decided to leave them.

He moved to the room where he'd penetrated the penthouse and fastened the vent cover back into place. There was a slight bulge that kept it from sitting true, but it wouldn't be noticed without a thorough investigation.

Bolan stayed to the shadows, listening for the triad assassin executioner to arrive. He didn't have to wait for long. The heavy doors opened with a clack and he heard a deep, resonant voice tell someone to put the bags away. From his vantage point, Bolan could see Augustyn, a tall, powerful man. He was wearing a chauffeur's uniform. The image that dying agent Reynolds had sent was of the man disguised as a servant. Taking off his formal hat, he fit Bolan's general appearance, over six feet in height, with wide powerful shoulders disappearing down into a slender waist, his torso a wedge of lean muscle. Black hair and blue eyes added to Augustyn's vague resemblance to the Executioner.

"Couldn't wait to get off the elevator to take charge again, eh, Wade?" an older man's voice croaked.

Augustyn chuckled, his shoulders visibly jerking. "I'm tired, *boss*," he said sarcastically.

He listened to the answering machine messages, and frowned. "Forget about the bags, Eugene. Fire up the computer and print out the tickets that Long sent."

"Tickets?" Eugene asked. "Right. I'll take care of it. Any idea where we're off to?"

"Darwin, Australia," Augustyn said. He wiped out the

two redundant digital messages and listened to his remaining messages. "Another cleaning job."

Eugene's disgust was broadcast in an audible grunt. He stepped into the open, and Bolan saw a man in his fifties, with salt-and-pepper hair, looking like an older version of Augustyn, only an inch or so shorter. An older brother? Bolan wondered at first, but then decided Augustyn had to have sought out someone with a close enough resemblance to pass for himself. "Cleaning means we've got more than one target," Eugene said.

"If I've got to meet with a local contact, there's going to be a laundry list of duties to carry out," Augustyn returned. "Not only a direct kill, but applying more pressure than they could bring on their own."

Eugene frowned. "This means a big, noisy mess. A deniable one to boot."

"That's why they're calling me in. Print the e-ticket. If you want, you can stay behind and make up for our lost time in Hong Kong," Augustyn replied. "They assume I travel alone anyhow, so you'd have to make your own way."

"No, thanks," Eugene replied. "I'd receive enough worried phone calls that I'd be stuck up the creek without a paddle if I took even another day away."

"You?" Augustyn chided.

"And you, too, by extension," Eugene amended, walking off.

The big assassin picked up a sleek cordless phone off the disklike answering machine and dialed a series of numbers. "Set up my usual Australia safari package. Darwin," he said.

Bolan skulked down a hallway and closed in on Eugene as he hovered over a keyboard, scanning through e-mail messages. The Executioner waited until the man hit the print command on the electronic ticket, then stepped into the den behind Augustyn's business manager. He jabbed a quick punch under Eugene's ear, a blow placed perfectly to render him unconscious. The businessman slumped into Bolan's arms, and he lowered the man on the floor. It took only a few moments to bind Eugene's wrists and ankles to keep him to the upcoming fight. He'd need more intelligence from the man later.

A sudden movement in Bolan's peripheral vision ignited his reflexes, throwing him to the floor an instant before the roar of a .45 split the air. The liquid crystal flat panel display for Augustyn's computer burst, a quarter-sized hole blown through it.

"You're good, whoever you are. I didn't even know you were in the apartment until I heard Eugene's grunt as you knocked him out," Augustyn said.

Bolan didn't answer. He had two alternate ways out of the office. One door to the right would force Augustyn to move more to intercept him, and it was close at hand. He shoved the desk chair toward that door and spun toward the farther exit from the den as another pair of .45-caliber slugs punched into the back of the chair.

As soon as he saw Augustyn disappear to intercept Bolan's false path, the Executioner exploded in the other direction, drawing his .45 in one swift movement. By the time the assassin discovered he'd been bluffed, it was too late for Augustyn to do anything except blow a chunk of wall apart with another big slug.

"Nice trick," Augustyn called out. Bolan heard him reload his half-depleted handgun. The Executioner remained silent, waiting for his opponent to reveal himself. Augustyn's chatter was meant to distract Bolan, covering noises. The way that the apartment was laid out, with soundproofed walls, there was no certain way to locate Augustyn by sound, though the noise of reloading or acquiring new weapons could be heard.

Bolan cursed himself for not taking down Eugene in a quieter manner, but the business manager was fit and brawny enough to turn a struggle into an extended wrestling match had he taken any other approach. Lethal force would have left Bolan behind the curve in figuring out what Augustyn had just been hired to do. Considering Eugene's voiced disgust, it had to be bad and he assumed a lot of people would die. Bolan had just declared war.

He looked down the hall to the corner and saw a reflective vase. He spotted Augustyn, observing the same curved, mirrored surface. Both men spotted each other at the same time, using the glassy surface to grant an around-the-corner view for defense. Bolan triggered the Norinco, blew the vase to splinters and retreated away from the intersection. Seeing another vase, he picked it up and hurled it toward the other end of the hallway. Crashing glass and an involuntary grunt of surprise told the Executioner that his distraction play worked and he nestled against the wall, crouched low and away from the edge so that he wouldn't be in hand-to-hand range if Augustyn whipped around the corner, prepared to disarm him.

Bullets punched into the wall, noise and fury rocking through the quiet calm of the apartment, but the gun battle's thunder was swallowed by Augustyn's nearly obsessive privacy measures. The Executioner waited a moment, but he didn't hear his enemy reload, and he knew that Augustyn had fallen back to flank him. Bolan turned and cut back toward the entrance to the apartment.

He was taking a chance, leaving Eugene at Augustyn's mercy, but as disposable as Bolan had assumed the manager was, the assassin would be loathe to get rid of a good asset just because the Executioner had dropped in on their little setup. If it appeared that Bolan was getting a decisive advantage, Augustyn might fall back and make the effort to take out the older man, but for now, the cocky killer assumed that on his own turf, he was unbeatable.

As Bolan entered the living room, he caught a glimpse of the tall, black-haired assassin and dived to the carpet as the rattle of a machine pistol cut through the air. Parabellum shockers snapped into the wall he'd been standing in front of only a brief moment before. Bolan returned fire, emptying the Norinco and pulling the suppressed Walther to keep up the heat until he reached the cover of the alcove. The Executioner's withering fire sent Augustyn packing into retreat, his autofire only resulting in damaged walls and shattered picture frames.

Bolan swiftly reloaded, shielded by Augustyn's sofa, but he realized his enemy had accessed a heavier supply of weapons. He'd been outgunned before, so it wasn't worth considering. Instead, he focused on what he could control. He looked into the kitchen, but a small mirror had been smashed, obscuring its ability to betray Augustyn's presence.

That was good news. Bolan's discovery of Augustyn's

corner views meant that the assassin was destroying his own means of detecting the Executioner's pursuit. It was a two-edged sword, and Bolan wasn't going to rush head-long into the kitchen in case Augustyn was laying in wait. Without grenades to clear the rooms of the penthouse, Bolan was going to have to take things slow and steady, using his senses to their utmost.

Just as he made this realization, the Executioner heard the familiar sound of the bounce of a grenade hitting car-pet. Bolan tucked down and cut loose with a loud roar, instants before the living room's atmosphere split apart in a peal of catastrophic noise. The shout saved his eardrums from the effect of the stun-shock grenade, and the bulk of the sofa protected him from the blazing glare of the mini-bomb's flash powder and shock wave. He pushed to his feet, already knowing what was coming next and he spot-ted Augustyn as a blur through the kitchen doorway, wielding a pair of long-bladed knives.

Bolan fired the Norinco, but the assassin was moving too quickly for a direct center mass shot. A .45-caliber slug sliced through Augustyn's side, slowing him and throwing off his pace. One of the nine-inch blades lashed down and rang violently against the slide of Bolan's .45, knocking it from his hands. Only the steel of the pistol had prevented Bolan's finger from being severed by the vicious slash, and he lunged in before the killer could fol-low up with the second knife. His shoulder-block took Au-gustyn in the breastbone and knocked him off balance, blowing breath from his lungs. Bolan wanted to unsnarl his Walther from where he'd pinned it between his oppo-nent's torso and himself, but with the glare of knife blades in his peripheral vision, he took the path of least resistance, hooking his emptied hand around and catching Augustyn over his ear.

The blow was meant to stop the assassin cold, but the savvy killer had seen it coming and tilted to one side, reducing the force from fatal to merely mind-reeling. The tip of one of the butcher knives flicked out and took Bolan across the bicep, a shallow cut, but one that forced the Executioner into a momentary retreat. Reflex had pulled him out of position for a shot with the Walther.

Bolan pulled the trigger anyway, the .32-caliber bullet exploding against the carpet next to Augustyn's head and distracted him enough so that the kick the assassin had been intending to launch missed shattering Bolan's jaw by mere millimeters. Another tug of the Walther's trigger elicited a grunt of pain, but it was answered by a second kick that took Bolan in the gut, staggering him backward.

Augustyn lunged, reaching for Bolan's fallen .45, but the Walther spoke again, a bullet chopping the frame of the Norinco and spinning it out of Augustyn's grasp.

"Son of a bitch!" Augustyn snarled. The knife whipped out of his hand as he threw it, the blade whirring so close it gouged a narrow furrow in Bolan's shoulder. He struggled to reach the .45, but Bolan lunged for the killer as he dived again for the big pistol. Their bodies crashed like great rams, paused in the air as the forces of their momentum struggled to overcome each other and then gravity pulled them to the floor.

Augustyn wrapped the fingers of one powerful hand around Bolan's throat, the grasp strong enough that the soldier felt the air cut off from his lungs, fingertips pressing against his carotid artery to deny his brain fresh blood. Bolan clamped one hand over Augustyn's bicep and punched hard into the assassin's elbow. Bone cracked like a gunshot, eliciting a wail of agony. The lethal pressure crushing his throat was gone, and Bolan saw that the hired killer's opposite shoulder had been wounded by the Walther, keeping Augustyn from using it to throttle Bolan. It was a small mercy that had saved Bolan's life.

The Executioner rammed a hard knee into Augustyn's breastbone, ejecting the breath from the man's lungs. He knuckle-punched the Hong Kong hit man in the Adam's apple and the assassin's eyes bulged as his throat collapsed under the brutal strike. His tongue lolled from his mouth and his wounded arm reached up to grab hold of Bolan's jacket. A second jutting-knuckle strike spiked between Augustyn's eyes, bone shattering under the force of the blow. The hit man fell limp with a full-body shudder.

Bolan cradled his aching knuckles. The blows had done their job, saving his life and ending that of a triad-hired murderer.

He staggered to his feet, retrieved the Norinco .45 and went to look for Eugene.

The Executioner had travel arrangements to make to meet with Augustyn's former employers.

2

Eugene Waylon's eyes fluttered open, and he felt the blood settling in his head. A cool breeze brushed through his hair, and as his vision focused, he could see Hong Kong's skyline. But it didn't quite look right. As his consciousness grew stronger, he realized that it was upside down. A grip like a vise held on to both ankles, and suddenly he slipped, dropping a foot. He looked around and saw the streets below, a blaze of garish neon ready to suck him down.

"Glad you could join me again," a grim and harsh voice said. Waylon tried to speak, but his throat had constricted in fear. His glasses slipped off his face and tumbled away, spiraling into the distance below. The businessman could feel his skin contracting all over his body, his stomach churning. Bile crept into the back of his throat.

"You don't need to know my name. You just need to know I exist." The voice cut into his terror. Waylon looked up to see the man's face. He looked as if he could have been Wade Augustyn's brother, except his blue eyes were even more chilling and penetrating.

"What do you want?" Waylon croaked, the sourness of his bile burning like a cloud of napalm through his mouth.

"The man you fronted for is dead," the Executioner said. "I'll be taking his place for a while, and when I'm done, I want you to fold up his operation and throw it away."

"What operation?"

Bolan released one of Waylon's ankles, which elicited a bleat of fear from him. He could see the arm still holding his ankle was wrapped in a bandage around the biceps. The businessman was able to see the raw power in Bolan's arms, but a smear of red grew in the center of the bandage.

"You can either quit playing stupid, or you can see how long I can hold you up with an injured arm," Bolan said.

"Wait! Wait!" Waylon howled. "Don't drop me!"

"Keep talking, Eugene," Bolan said.

"All right, I'll make Augustyn's assassination operation disappear," Waylon conceded. "Just don't let go."

Bolan took hold of Waylon's other ankle. "Before making it disappear, e-mail all the details to the address I wrote down on your computer desk. All of his contacts, everyone who supplied him, everyone who contracted him."

Waylon nodded. "Yes."

"Which triad was Augustyn working for?" Bolan asked.

"The Black Rose," Waylon answered.

Bolan knew the organization. They were a particularly aggressive and brutal group, given to bouts of violent infighting. "If I hear you've set yourself up as someone else's front man, I'll make you wish I dropped you off this roof," Bolan told him. "I'l be watching your every move."

"Yes, sir," Waylon said.

"But first, tell me who Augustyn would use as his supplier for an operation in Darwin, Australia," Bolan ordered.

Waylon looked up. "He'd kill me if I gave him up."

Bolan pulled Waylon up farther. Eye-level with the balcony, he could see Augustyn's corpse. "You really think he'll ever take a shot at you?" Bolan asked.

"N-no, sir," Waylon stammered.

"Your choice. Spill your guts, or I spill you into the street and take everything apart the hard way," Bolan said.

Waylon began to talk. He was grateful to be dragged onto the balcony and thrown atop Augustyn's clammy, pulped form, despite the splatter of blood from the assassin's caved-in face that spurted over his clothes. He dragged himself away from the corpse and looked to Bolan, who had a laptop sitting on the table.

"What's that for?" Waylon asked.

"Paying your debt to society," Bolan informed him.

"Listen, I was just Augustyn's business manager. I never pulled a trigger!" Waylon said.

"I know. You're still covered in stains from your blood money, however," Bolan replied. "Get to work."

Waylon sat behind the keyboard and saw the screen contained Augustyn's private, Cayman Island bank accounts. "What do I do?"

"Empty them," Bolan said.

"But, how will I live?" Waylon asked.

The Executioner lifted his Norinco .45. "Without a hole in one side of your skull and a grapefruit-sized excavation cavity on the other."

"Okay," Waylon answered.

"You're in charge of that killer's legitimate business holdings. Manage them well, and make your money. Continue his role as philanthropist and run his companies well," Bolan continued. "If your businesses fail and people suffer and go out of work, I'll be back."

Waylon nodded.

"Open these accounts and transmit to this array," Bolan told him, putting down a piece of paper. "Empty the coffers."

Waylon glanced at Augustyn's fortune. Hundreds of millions of dollars in several accounts were going to be transferred to the set of banks Bolan had put before him. He looked questioningly toward the Executioner. "This was a robbery?"

"This was eliminating pure evil," Bolan stated. "However, his blood money will be put to use for some good."

"In your pocket?" Waylon asked.

Bolan shook his head no, disdain for the thought registering in a hard, chilling glare. The money from assets acquired while Bolan was on missions would have made Bolan one of the richest men in the world. But Bolan had no interest in such things. The money would be used by Stony Man Farm to fund future missions.

Waylon finished transferring Augustyn's funds. "I'm sorry."

"For what?" Bolan asked.

"For assuming that money was your motivation," Waylon stated, obviously trying to get back on Bolan's good side.

The Executioner shook his head.

"It wasn't Augustyn's, either," Waylon continued. "He did it for the thrill."

"That's not my goal, either," Bolan warned. "Don't think too hard about it, Eugene. This is the end of your old life. Now's your chance to be a saint and wash the grime off your soul."

The businessman nodded and watched as the big black .45 went into Bolan's hip holster.

"Grow old gracefully, Eugene," Bolan said. "And you'll never see me again."

With that, the Executioner left the lavish penthouse, just as the sun cracked the skyline.

BOLAN TOOK THE TIME to dispose of the guns in Augustyn's apartment. He didn't want anyone in the Hong Kong underworld to get hold of the assassin's rather impressive firepower. He had gone to an auto yard and hidden the submachine guns, rifles and handguns he'd stolen from the triad assassin inside the trunk of a car on the pile to be crushed and compressed into a cube of scrap metal. He would have liked to have set some of the arsenal aside for himself, including the new .338 Lapua Magnum-chambered Barrett rifle. The big gun was a state-of-the-art antipersonnel weapon that would give a marksman a reach of a mile.

He'd have to find something in Darwin from Augustyn's supplier.

Bolan waited an hour, and as soon as the magnet dropped the arsenal-packed junk mobile into the compressor, he left. He could hear the grinding of metal into a fused, crushed block. He got into his rental car and drove to the airport, where the electronic ticket would ferry him to Darwin, Australia.

He pulled his phone from his pocket in response to its subtle thrumming vibration, and flipped it open to hear Barbara Price, Stony Man's mission controller, on the other end.

"You're not coming home?" Price asked.

"I've got some unexpected business. I'll be extending my trip," Bolan answered.

"Striker, we've got a few operations waiting on the back burner here at home," Price told him. "You're not even certain what Augustyn had been hired for."

"He was hired to be an exterminator. And these aren't vermin he'd been called in on, these are human beings," Bolan explained. "If they're people I normally would have targeted, then good. I'll do the job, and then take out Augustyn's paymasters."

"And if they're citizens in the way of the triads?" Price asked.

"Then I just burn down the gangsters," Bolan stated. "I'll come home even faster."

"Be careful down there, Striker," Price said.

"I'll take care of things and keep you posted," Bolan replied, hanging up.

Bolan considered the situation. No one in Darwin would be prepared for an all-out power play by the triads, and no naval blockade or aircraft carrier offshore could calm this conflict.

It required the Executioner's touch of cleansing fire.

BOBBY YEUNG STEPPED OUT of the back of the Ford Explorer once his bodyguards had determined that the area for the next five hundred yards was empty of human habitation except for the police and fire officers looking at the burned-out ranch house. The sheriff, Ansen Crown, noticed him and walked over.

"What's the story?" Yeung asked as Crown approached him.

The sheriff looked around, then shook his head. "Arson. No bodies found."

Yeung nodded. He restrained his frustration as he realized that the rednecks he'd hired had been sloppy. Obwe "Grandfather" Wangara was one of the last men alive among the tribes with the determination to expose the Black Rose Triad's operations in their territories.

"You heard about the girl boarding the bus to Alice Springs, right?" Crown asked.

Yeung nodded. Wangara's granddaughter, Arana, was missing from the ashes of the fire. A lone, eighteen-year-old Aboriginal girl would be hard to find in the outback. If she reached any authorities Yeung's triad had not paid off, there would be difficulties.

Killing native people in a remote location of Australia was one thing. Dealing with government officials in the open would be another. Yeung wished that the Black Rose Triad's assassin would respond and pick up his electronic ticket. While he was irate with the men he'd hired locally, he knew that the triad assassin was trustworthy. The man had been a powerful, secret asset. His very appearance turned attention away from the organization he worked for, as the triads were notoriously loathe to use non-Chinese in their employ.

"Just make certain that no one raises a stink about the old man's home burning. If possible, report him dead," Yeung stated.

"I've got everything hushed up," Crown answered. "But without a body—"

Yeung interrupted, holding his frustration in check. "Do what you can. I've got a troubleshooter coming in to help out with this."

"I can pass most of this off on bigots getting drunk and riled, but an organized assassin…" Crown began.

"If you had done your job the way I wanted you to, none of this would have been necessary. Since you couldn't evict these people, just be glad I need a mouthpiece among local law enforcement. Otherwise, we'd be using your bones as that old man," Yeung snapped. "Got that?"

Crown clenched his jaw but nodded in quiet agreement.

"Don't fuck with me. I know where you live," Yeung snarled. He turned and got back in his SUV. His cell phone warbled and he plucked it from his pocket.

"Bobby, our man picked up his ticket and boarded his flight." The call was from Frankie Law, his right-hand man. "Our troubles are over."

"I'd like to think so, Frankie," Yeung replied. "But the situation's just gotten a little more complicated. The Abos who were straining at the leash finally slipped out of sight. At least one of them is on the way to civilization."

"I'll get our boys on the street. What's the description?" Law asked.

"Five feet, black, about eighteen. Fairly cute for a little black girl," Yeung stated.

"Damn, not the chick," Law said.

"You've got a problem with that?" Yeung inquired.

"I just wanted a little taste. She was nicer than you let on," Law replied.

"Find her and kill her when you're done," Yeung ordered. "These fuckers have given me enough headaches. "Just find the little bitch and deliver her head to me. Keep the rest for whatever you want."

"Kinky." Law chuckled.

"Dammit, Frankie!" Yeung said. It was too late. His head man in Darwin had hung up.

Yeung put the phone away, looking out the window.

When he'd been asked to set up a major transportation hub and processing center for the triad's heroin pipeline, Yeung had jumped at the chance. It would be his ticket to the top of the heap in Hong Kong. Now, a year later, he was sick of the outback, sick of the Aborigines and the ugly, inbred whites with their mush-mouthed butchering of the English language, and he was sick of being stuck on the ass of the planet. He was a city boy. He wanted to be back among skyscrapers and neon lights and bodies packed together like sardines, with loud music, cigarette smoke and perfumed whores jammed in around him, pawing over his senses.

The facility was operating at half capacity, but once it was running at full power, he'd be called back to Hong Kong to be given an opportunity to rise up the ladder.

All it would take would be a few more dead Aborigines, and he would have the facility operating with impunity.

He was glad that the triad's assassin was coming to fix it all.

3

Bolan got off the plane, eyes sharp for the presence of any members of the Black Rose Triad who would be at the airport to greet him. If they knew Wade Augustyn by sight, they would know something was wrong. His carry-on was only loaded with clothes. He'd be unarmed in the face of a mobster offensive. Under other circumstances that wouldn't be a problem, but in an airport full of civilians, any delay in neutralizing armed opposition would increase the risk of bystanders being gunned down.

Since no Chinese gunmen popped out of the woodwork, Berettas blazing, Bolan felt secure going to the public lockers. He felt under the one he'd been directed to in the attachment to the e-mail containing the electronic ticket he'd ridden in on. The key was taped under a metal lip, and he plucked it free. Inside the locker were two envelopes. One was a large manila, stuffed with what looked like a file. The other was a smaller padded envelope containing a cellular phone. Bolan tucked the file into his carry-on and retrieved the phone. He hit the speed dial.

"Finally made it," came the voice on the other end.

"I was just getting back from other business," Bolan said, imitating Augustyn's voice.

When Bobby Yeung spoke again, he gave no indication of noting any difference. "Say no more. How long will it take for you to get equipped for your safari?"

"Give me till dusk to get what I need," Bolan said.

"Good. We've got a situation. We might need you prowling in Darwin first. I've got my people out and about, but…"

Bolan walked over to a table in the concourse food court and took a seat. He pulled out the file and set it before him, opening it. "There's a picture of them in my file?"

"Naturally," the Black Rose man said.

"Which one?" Bolan asked.

"The girl. She escaped, and we need to put her down fast."

"You can't find her?" Bolan pressed. He looked at the young woman. She was pretty, with big beautiful brown eyes. The name scrawled in the margin of the photo was Arana Wangara. It was right next to a photograph of an older man labeled Grandfather Wangara. In red marker, across Grandfather's face, was written Troublemaker.

"She disappeared in Alice Springs. We had hoped to catch up with her, but—"

"But they didn't think that she could blend in with a crowd because she was just an Abo, right?"

The Chinese mobster chuckled. Bolan's derision of his people's bigoted arrogance wasn't lost on him. "It wasn't my people. We'd had a couple of thick-headed whites doing the legwork. I'll have some real talent searching the bus stations in Darwin—including you."

"If you've got your act together, what do you need me for?" Bolan asked.

"Because I'm still stuck in the middle of absolute nowhere. And I need someone smart making sure this little chickie is put down," the triad spokesman said.

"I don't do bus station detail," Bolan replied. "Even in Australia, there's too much of a urine smell."

"How about you roll up a few thousand yen and stick them up your damn nose to filter out the piss-stink?" the Chinese bartered.

"A few thousand yen's pocket change," Bolan countered.

"Dollars?" the gangster offered.

"Pounds sterling," Bolan said.

"You're killin' me!" Yeung exclaimed.

"You should be so important," Bolan warned. "Come to think of it, why are we killing a young woman?"

"Because she's a liability," the mobster explained, sounding as if he were talking to a child.

"Well, if you want me to bust my ass for a week hunting down Grandpa Abo, you're paying by the day," Bolan reminded him. "Frankly, I'd rather make my job easier."

The Chinese man hissed in frustration. "Can you get this kind of information out of the girl?"

"Only if she stays alive," Bolan admonished. "And stays healthy."

"Healthy," the mob boss repeated.

"As in untouched. If she goes catatonic because some of your boys took a piece, my work is going to be a lot harder. And they personally won't like me when I have to work harder," Bolan growled. "Got it?"

"You kill my men—"

"What? You called me in because you couldn't handle this. What makes you think you can handle me?" Bolan asked. "Because if you can handle me, some old man shouldn't be the top page of your hit list."

"That's because they say he's one of their shaman... whatevers. He walks in the Dreamtime or some such. Keeping up with him is impossible," Yeung answered.

"You called me in to exterminate fifteen unarmed Aboriginal activists," Bolan said.

"They're not Chinese. What do we care?"

"You got me. As long as I get my cash," Bolan replied.

"I'll get a message to my boys," Bobby Yeung replied. "You'll get your bonus for catching the girl."

Bolan hung up the phone and examined the files after getting something to drink at one of the counters on the food court.

From the description of the targets, it didn't take the Executioner long to figure out that the triads were clearing a tract of land for a large facility, and the heads on the list were community activists trying to maintain their tribal lands. Considering the space being opened up by the Chinese mobsters, Bolan wouldn't have put it past them to build an airport that would be a stopover to "sanitize" overseas shipments, a form of relay that would keep customs from looking too closely at repackaged contraband.

It was a perfect setup for anything from knockoff goods to drugs. Remembering his basic knowledge of the Australian outback, and the fact that he was going to clean house a hundred or so miles from the famous Uluru mound, he'd be operating in a desert environment. The file requested that everything be made to look as if it were the act of a lone psychotic with a powerful hunting rifle.

Bolan finished his drink, bought a sandwich wrap to go and switched to the cell phone he had taken from Eugene Waylon. It was programmed with Augustyn's Darwin contacts.

He flipped open the phone, and typed in a quick text message to the assassin's arms dealer in northern Australia. The response was immediate.

"Meet me in a half an hour." An address was provided with the response. Bolan pocketed the phone and went to a shop for some items he knew he'd need for the upcoming meeting with the gun seller. It'd have to be enough until he got his hands on some real firearms.

ARANA WANGARA GOT OFF the bus and kept her head low. She tried to blend in as a bored teenage tourist, keeping sullenly to herself as she tucked her knapsack tightly under her arm. Wangara scanned the crowd for signs of the Asian musclemen working for the mobsters who'd ordered her home torched.

She'd loaded a couple of rocks in the bottom of her bag as a crude weapon. The weighted sack would at least knock a bad guy off his feet, if not break a jaw or cheekbone. It wasn't a shotgun, but at least it was something. Seeing her unarmed might actually lull her hunters into a false sense of security that would give her a chance to upgrade to an actual firearm.

Wangara clutched the strap of her bag tightly, eyes darting. Her grandfather had taught her how to use his rifle, a bolt-action Enfield from World War II, original

ANZAC issue, and a pump shotgun. She'd even taken lives, dropping a marauding, sheep-killing dingo with the Enfield, as well as wild hogs. She'd learned that she could kill to protect lives, and while there was a difference between Chinese gangsters or bigoted Outback rednecks and a feral dog, the end result was the same.

Violence against violence, to preserve life, she thought. If she fell, then the gangsters and their hired thugs would kill other members of the tribe to keep them silent about the activities on their stolen land. She certainly did not want to die, but she also knew living would be made hollow if she let down her grandfather.

Wangara tucked her chin down against her chest and continued through the bus terminal, weaving in time with the crowd around her. Someone on the periphery of the group jerked his attention toward her, the sudden movement focusing Wangara like a laser on him. It was a young Asian man, wearing black sunglasses and a battered leather jacket too large for his slight frame, but with enough drape to hide a pair of sawed-off shotguns under its folds. She returned to staring at the floor, walking quickly to keep pace with the other tourists.

The young Chinese man tried to push through the throng of departing bus riders, but Wangara was out the door and turning down the street. There was another Asian man outside, this one wearing an overly large jacket, except in denim. He reached under his lapel, watching her through his impenetrable shades. Wangara fought not to run, not to look at the gunman out of the corner of her eye.

Acknowledgment of her hunters would give them the advantage. They were holding back, not quite sure if she was the prey they were seeking. If she bolted, or even if she glared at them too long to study them, they would be certain and act quickly to either restrain her or just pull their guns and fill her with holes.

Wangara kept to the main street. The gangsters would be hesitant to act in the open, with so many witnesses around. The reason she was being hunted was to keep the triad's scheme from being discovered. The blatant, public assassination of a young woman on the run from her Aboriginal tribal lands would draw attention like a lightning rod.

The man with the denim jacket pulled out a cell phone and spoke into it. He turned it toward her, and Wangara knew she couldn't suddenly look away, despite the fact that she knew he was using the cell's camera attachment. She only hoped that the usually blurry distance shots would make her identification difficult, especially since the young mob tough was only able to catch an angled profile.

It wasn't much, but she was grateful for any advantage she had. The weight of the rocks in the bag on her shoulder gave her more reassurance, but nothing would last forever. Sooner or later, the man in the jean jacket would move in to make a final identification, and Wangara would have to fight or die.

She hoped that her grandfather was right about the lone crusader.

THE EXECUTIONER STOOD in the doorway of Red's Sporting Supply, his eyes adjusting to the light.

"Plastic surgery again?"

Bolan scanned the small sporting goods store and saw

an older man with a rust-colored crew cut and a nose that had been mashed flat in countless fights. Dark, hard eyes glared out from under a beetle brow as he evaluated the newcomer.

Bolan nodded.

"You're paranoid, Wade," Red said. "Come in the back."

"Sure," Bolan replied, adopting Wade's speech patterns, but speaking softly.

"What'd you do to your throat?" the arms supplier asked.

"Had the surgeon give it a few scrapes," Bolan explained. "Change my voice just enough. Figured a new face isn't any good without an altered voice."

"Like I said, Wade. Paranoid."

Bolan smiled. "I'm still alive."

Red laughed as they entered the back room. There was a door and from the other side, Bolan could hear muffled pops coming through a basement stairwell entrance. Signs on the windows out front had mentioned a public range, firearms rentals, as well as a storage fee for personally owned weapons. "I've got a bag ready for you, based on what you texted me."

Bolan nodded and walked over to the gym bag with the All Blacks logo on the side. He unzipped it, looking at a pair of pistol rugs and a short rifle case.

"The rifle's been broken down, but if you want to look at it, I'll let you check it out on the range," Red said. He tossed Bolan a pair of ear protectors and some shooting glasses.

Bolan donned them and took the bag to the basement range.

"Won't be able to sight in at a distance," Red said, following him down, wearing his own ear and eye protection.

"I know how to zero based on close range," Bolan replied as he opened the case. He assembled the weapon, recognizing it as a VEPR. Considering that the VEPR was a reengineered RPK machine gun, itself a derivative of the AK-47, the Executioner knew it would be a good, tough rifle, immune to any hostile environment he'd drag it through. He looked at the magazine and saw that it was chambered for .300 Winchester Magnum rounds. The rifle's reinforced receiver could handle the extra-powerful cartridge. Whereas the AK itself had been made from stamped steel, the VEPR was made of stronger metal, with a stronger bolt, designed for firing prolonged bursts from extended light-machine-gun-sized magazines. On single shot, it would handle the .300 Magnum rounds just fine. The wooden AK furniture had been replaced by desert camouflage reinforced fiberglass. He attached a scope and test fired. With the rifle set to a "point-blank" of 200 yards, at a mere 25 yards he knew how high the first shot should hit. The test impact was within millimeters of Bolan's estimation, and he reset the scope.

The balance was almost perfect, though the shoulder stock was a little short for his long arms. It would do, he thought, and looked to Red.

"If you're going to pretend to be Wade, you should be a little more finicky," the store owner said.

Bolan tensed.

"Don't worry. You're still a paying customer, but you should realize, Eugene contacted me," Red stated.

"So why aren't you worried about me?" Bolan asked, using his normal voice.

Red pointed to the bag. "Because if you were going to try to kill me, there's enough weaponry in there to take me and my boys out."

Bolan was aware that the other two shooters on the line had stopped firing and were glancing at him.

"You could have given me dummy ammunition," Bolan stated. "Or sealed off the rounds in separate containers, like you did with the rifle."

"The magazines for the pistols are empty," Red explained. "But even so, you've got a pair of good working knives in there. If you're good enough to take down Wade in hand-to-hand, the revolver in my pocket wouldn't be worth much against you." The black-market dealer pulled a small Smith & Wesson Centennial from his pocket and set it on a counter.

"You're right. I am a paying customer. And the only reason I'd mix it up with you and your boys would be if you made a move against me," Bolan stated honestly.

"Face-to-face, you're very convincing. Good acting," Red complimented him. "But if Eugene has blown your cover to me…"

"He might try to contact the Black Rose Triad and let them know that I'm not the man they hired," Bolan said. "I'd hoped to give him a chance to go straight."

"Wade hired Eugene because the twerp is the same type of soulless bastard that he was," Red explained. "You just cleared the deck for Eugene to take charge of all Wade's assets, and maybe even hire a replacement for him."

"So what's your interest in warning me about all this?" Bolan asked.

"I don't do a lot of illicit business," the arms dealer replied. "I try to sell to otherwise law-abiding folks who know they can't count on a government to guard them. A lot of the time, it's guns for folks going to someplace really dangerous, like Jakarta, the Philippines or Thailand, where the thugs don't care about gun-control laws and are just looking for white-skinned Aussies because they know we're soft prey."

Bolan nodded. "Wade was an aberration?"

"He had the goods on me. He passed himself off as a stand-up guy, and after he made a couple of kills, he kept the weapons and the bill of sale. If I held out on him, he'd let the government know, and they'd shut me down cold," Red told him. "My arse was on the line."

"So you never got paid," Bolan said.

"I was paid a token amount, enough to keep me implicated in newer hits he performed with the stuff I gave him," Red answered. "The paper trail would sink me."

Bolan nodded. "I'll see what I can do."

"How do you know I'm not giving you a cock-and-bull?" Red asked.

"Because you know I'm not the type to just hand you over to the law," Bolan answered.

He checked the contents of the pistol rugs. One contained a 9 mm Walther P-99 QA. The polymer-framed pistol was flat, and had interchangeable back straps for its grip and felt good in Bolan's hand. He popped the medium-sized grip and put in the extra-large version. The P-99's Quick Action trigger was a relatively light double-action pull, feeling more like a Glock than anything. The smooth, straight pull provided antiflinch safety but was light enough for fine accuracy. Despite its light weight and compact size, the weapon still held sixteen rounds in its magazine with another pill in the chamber. The barrel was threaded, and there was a sound suppressor for the smaller handgun. "I didn't have a PPK for Wade…"

"That's okay. I like this," Bolan answered.

The other pistol rug held a long-barreled .44 Magnum Raging Bull revolver, by Taurus. It was an acceptable substitute for the Executioner's usual Desert Eagle. Bolan dry-fired, testing the trigger pull. It was as smooth as butter, and Bolan didn't doubt that the mass of the revolver would soak up recoil as easily as the gas mechanism of his preferred Desert Eagle.

"I smoothed out all the linkages but didn't change the pull weight," Red explained. "It'll pop any of its caps reliably, once you return the firing pin to operation."

"If I were going for a snatch and grab, I'd plop a few shells into the revolver and start shooting. Smart man."

"No. Paranoid myself…and like you said, I'm still alive."

"Alive, and richer," Bolan said. "Where's the firing pin?"

Red tossed him a small plastic bag. The Executioner replied by handing him a thick roll of money.

"You don't need to," the store owner said.

"I pay my own way," Bolan stated.

Red nodded. "Eugene might try to do something to take care of me when he finds out I didn't burn you down."

Bolan took out his cell phone, sending a quick e-mail

off to Stony Man Farm. "I'll make arrangements that will shield you. Congratulations on becoming a confidential informant for the United States Justice Department. You're involved in a sting to take down a killer for hire."

Red raised an eyebrow. "Against Eugene Waylon?"

Bolan nodded.

"So anything he says will be ignored by the authorities?" Red asked. "What if he turns the triad onto me?"

"That won't be a problem," Bolan told him. He'd already installed the firing pin in the Raging Bull revolver and loaded it with six rounds. He zipped it back into its pistol rug. "I'm here to make certain of that. All of Augustyn's loose ends, including Waylon, will be taken care of."

He began setting up the Walther and its shoulder holster. "Just be sure to stay on your toes until I contact you that everything is in the clear," Bolan said, thumbing rounds into the P-99.

"No kidding," Red replied. He put the Centennial back in his pocket. "Good luck, Mr...."

Bolan shook his head. "Luck has nothing to do with it. And the less you know, the better."

Red held out his hand, and the two men shook. Bolan explored the Australian's eyes for signs of deceit, finding nothing. Not like the terrified traitor he'd left behind in Hong Kong.

EUGENE WAYLON KNEW that it wouldn't take the big bastard long to meet up with Red. He'd toyed with the idea of calling the Darwin police department to let them know about an arms deal going down in their backyard, but he knew the cops might not be enough to take down the man who'd reduced Wade Augustyn to a bloody pulp in the middle of his own living room.

Besides, calling the police wasn't in Waylon's repertoire. He did get on the horn, however. Not to the Chinese. If the Black Rose Triad had learned that their safe, sanitized Western assassin was permanently out of action and replaced by a fake, Waylon knew that his own life would be forfeit.

He decided to get in touch with the men Augustyn sometimes called in for backup. There were four of them, members of a U.S. Marine detachment who had gone AWOL in the Philippines when they had come under suspicion of hiring themselves out to local gangsters as muscle. Going into hiding, the former Marines simply expanded their moonlighting activities for the Filipino mobsters to become full-fledged mercenaries. As hired guns, they were among the best, well-trained marksmen, and a disciplined fire team. The renegades' escape had squashed the Marines' and Navy's efforts to make an example of them.

Waylon heard Garrett Victor's gruff voice as the squad leader picked up. "What?"

"It's Waylon. I've got work for you," the businessman said. "Where are you?"

"Kickin' back in Sydney," Victor replied. "Having fun. Wade need help?"

"He needs avenging," Waylon corrected.

"What the fuck?" Victor growled.

"Someone killed him, and he's now going on an operation in Darwin," Waylon explained. "I need this bastard taken down, preferably without the Black Rose finding out."

"Why not get the triad to take this mook down?" Victor asked.

Waylon sighed. "And let them know that their number-one foreign asset has been compromised?"

"He's still going to be dead. They give you another job…"

"How'd you like some fat triad money, Gar?" Waylon asked. "You and the boys living higher on the hog, and you won't have to pull grunt work like sitting on a cargo freighter, chasing off pirates."

Waylon could hear the gears turning in the greedy mercenary's brain.

"This guy took out Wade, though," Victor stated. "He's obviously bad news."

"That's why I'm calling you and the boys," Waylon explained. "The four of you could outfight anyone."

"It'll take us a while to get a flight to Darwin."

"I'll arrange it all for you. You can pick up the tickets at the counter," Waylon informed him. "Do I have you on board, or do I have to look elsewhere for someone with balls?"

"Nobody tells me I ain't got balls, Eugene," Victor snarled. "I'll rouse the boys and we'll bring this fucker's head to you."

Waylon smiled, and told them at which airline they could pick up their tickets.

With a group of easily goaded, overly macho thugs like these four, Eugene Waylon could not only recover from the loss of Augustyn, but continue living in the style he was accustomed to.

But first things first. The tall man in black was going to have to die.

4

Bolan's cell phone vibrated in his pocket and he plucked it out.

"We've got a sighting on the girl," Bobby Yeung said. "I've got a man on her tail, but he's holding back, as per your instructions."

"Good," Bolan replied. He pushed away his dinner plate and snapped his fingers for the waitress to bring his check. The efficiency of the Chinese gangsters was excellent, and Bolan knew he'd only needed to wait until they had spotted Arana Wangara. "No contact until I arrive."

"You've got it," Yeung answered. "The address is in text format."

Bolan looked at it. He'd picked a small diner in the general neighborhood of the Darwin bus station, and Wangara's location was only a few blocks away, according to the tiny GPS map screen on his phone. The waitress arrived and Bolan paid her, leaving twice as much for her tip than his meal cost.

"Keep the change," Bolan told her and he left the restaurant, his jacket hanging loosely over his broad shoulders. Its billowing folds hid the Walther P-99 hanging in its shoulder holster. No bulge was visible, despite the fact that the weapon's blunt suppressor was still attached.

Having memorized Wangara's last reported position on the GPS screen, he made a beeline, altering his course to get ahead of the Aboriginal woman. Bolan didn't want to spook her, and he knew if he took custody of her, with the Chinese gunmen alongside him, he would never be able to win her trust. The Executioner figured he needed at least a minute of privacy to explain his ruse to her, otherwise there was a good possibility that he'd be forced into a gunfight with the gangsters.

A shootout would blow Bolan's cover with the Black Rose Triad, and potentially draw the attention of the law. Kurtzman had been able to finesse new background information for the gun dealer in order to provide Red with some cushion, and to keep tighter observation on him. The cyber expert had given Bolan a heads-up that Waylon was making calls over a heavily encrypted line. Augustyn's paranoia had been such that he had tight security on his cell phone and Waylon's. With a constantly morphing encryption key, it took even the Farm's awesome computer resources more than a minute to break each phone call, and Waylon's phone discipline was strict, hanging up before Kurtzman could determine the contents or the recipients of the call.

It was one of the reasons the Executioner had stopped off at a grocery store and bought some duct tape and a heavy-spined butcher's knife as soon as he left the airport. Tucked under his shirt in a duct tape and cardboard sheath, the butcher's knife was invisible under his waistband, but the foot-long blade had the power to punch through bone and heavy muscle. Two paring knives strapped to his forearms were backups, their blunt, triangular points making them good throwing weapons once he popped off their handles, turning them into front-heavy darts. With the tape-fashioned forearm sheaths, he could have whipped out the improvised throwing knives and planted them in the throats of whatever gunmen were backing Red's play.

The fact that Red hadn't sprung a trap on him was the only reason the Executioner hadn't exploded into a flash of bloody action and taken his head off with the butcher's knife. Restraint had saved the Australian black marketeer's life, as well as those of his henchmen. Of course, Red's honesty had only confirmed Bolan's suspicions. He would have to return to Hong Kong to deal with the lying, traitorous Waylon.

Since visiting Red, Bolan's improvised combat knives were supplanted. He'd put the butcher's knife away and had replaced it with a Gerber LMF Bowie to back up his 9 mm handgun.

Bolan moved at a steady pace, mindful of appearing too aggressive. Wangara, having been stalked halfway across the continent, would be on edge, and if he approached her like a bull, she'd turn and run like hell. He didn't need that, either. A six-foot-plus white man chasing a young Aboriginal woman through the streets would also attract unneeded attention.

He spotted Wangara, her head tucked down, white earbuds dangling around her neck. Her knapsack looked lumpy and heavy, as if it were packed with rocks rather than clothes. The Executioner realized she wasn't going to be a pushover if anyone stepped up to her and tried anything rough. Picking up his pace, he caught up with her and slowed to match her stride. It took a few moments for her to notice him, but he was too close for her to pull down her bag and swing it to crack his head.

"Don't make a scene, Arana," Bolan said softly, almost soothingly. "I know you're being chased. The people after you think I'm working for them."

She looked up at him, brown eyes wide and fearful. The young woman took a sidestep, and only ended up bouncing against a storefront. Bolan rested his hand on her shoulder, pinning her shoulder strap in place to defang her. "I'm not looking for a fight. In fact, I don't want you hurt at all," he said.

Wangara looked at the hand on her shoulder, then longingly at her knapsack. She pursed her lips and sighed. "I came here looking for help. Those Chinese destroyed my home."

"I figured as much," Bolan answered. "I want you alive and safe. That means you have to pretend that you're frightened of me."

Wangara glanced up at him. "That won't be difficult."

The Executioner nodded. They stopped walking and Bolan checked on the two Black Rose Triad soldiers on their tail. They were closing in, relaxed. One had a smug smirk on his face, glad that they had finally gotten their job done. "Just stay close," he said.

"I figured I was in for a rough time," Wangara said calmly.

"You're safe from that for now," Bolan told her, taking

her knapsack. He opened it and saw three heavy rocks. "I just need to ditch these two."

Wangara looked at him and took a step back. "Why?"

Bolan grabbed her wrist tightly and tugged her closer. The move looked harsher than it felt. Bolan didn't want to seem too accommodating of the young woman in front of the gangsters, but he measured the amount of force he used perfectly. "Stay close," he repeated.

Looking back to the Chinese mobsters, he saw them slow, looks of doubt crossing their features. A deft turn of his head allowed Bolan to see what was up. A van slowed, the side panel rolled back and men in black sat perched to leap out. Bolan yanked Wangara off her feet and twisted, throwing himself through the plate-glass window of a clothing store, his broad shoulders smashing the glass and shielding the woman from shards and splinters. As his feet cleared the hole he'd created, he heard the crack of handguns filling the air. Bolan and the young woman struck the floor as bullets popped above their heads, the high velocity creating miniature sonic booms that crackled in the Executioner's ears.

He pushed Wangara against the base of the wall with one hand, the other pulling the Walther from its shoulder leather in one swift movement. "Stay down!" he shouted.

Bolan rolled to one knee, the 9 mm pistol leading the way. He spotted a handgun-wielding Chinese man gaping at the broken window, wondering at the blur of motion that had snatched his target out of the way. The Executioner milked the trigger twice. Bullets tore into the chest of the gunman, the shooter's dying reflex jerking him back toward the panel van, forcing his allies to stumble as they tried to get out of the vehicle.

Bolan swept his Walther to a second gunman and punched a single 9 mm pill through his ear. The Asian marauder tumbled face-first to the concrete, eliciting a cry of dismay from the van's driver. A third and a fourth gunman exploded through the open side panel, spreading out in response to Bolan's marksmanship. The Executioner dropped and rolled on his shoulders as a shotgun belched violently. A clothing rack above him jerked and billowed under the 12-gauge assault, pellets shredding fabric, hangers clanking on metal tubing. People in the store screamed in fear, but Bolan's explosive entry had driven them to cover. No one had been struck by gunfire yet, except the attackers.

The Executioner completed his shoulder roll and came up in a half-crouch, the Walther popping out sound-suppressed 9 mm slugs into the face of the shotgunner. Bolan's first shot struck the Chinese gunman in the nose, disintegrating it and producing a gory tunnel in the middle of his face. The second round drilled into the Chinese shooter's left eye. The dead man tumbled across a garbage can, toppling it as the weight deformed the metal mesh. The shotgun clattered in the street, but the last gunman cut loose with his pistol.

As with almost anyone in a combat situation, the Chinese shooter's initial shots went high, 9 mm holes shattering craters in a mirror. Bolan stepped to the side, his Walther blazing and pumping rounds into the gunman's chest, a trio of bullets burning through the gangster's heart.

The van's engine revved, and the Executioner whirled, hammering another shot into the front window. The van veered off course, rolling up onto the curb, and Bolan vaulted through the shattered storefront window, reaching for the door. The driver twisted, trying to get out of his seat as his hand dropped to a handgun in his waistband. Bolan tore the door open and lashed out with the butt of the Walther, the sleek pistol's reinforced frame cracking across the driver's jaw.

Stunned, the getaway man was helpless as Bolan plucked the revolver from his waistband. He glanced to one side and saw that one of the two men who had been sent to meet with him was back on his feet. The other clutched his chest, face twisted in pain.

"Get him over here!" Bolan ordered. He turned to the driver and clubbed him again, this shot aimed at the wheelman's temple. The man slumped out of his seat like a sack of laundry.

Bolan looked back and noticed Wangara, peering over the bottom of the broken window, her face a mask of terror as she observed the carnage the Executioner had wrought. "Get in the back," he said.

She opened her mouth to complain, but Bolan's gaze turned hard. "In!"

Wangara got up, stepped through the window and ran to the back of the van in a moment. Bolan met the triad pair halfway and helped the wounded man into the back.

"Drive," Bolan ordered the healthy gangster as he slammed the side panel shut.

"Where?" the man asked.

"Someplace safe. I'll help your buddy while you're driving," Bolan told him. He tore open the wounded man's bloody shirt. The bullet had struck him high in the chest, and from the color of the dark red blood, he knew that it hadn't severed a major artery. "Don't speed. We don't need cops on our case," he said.

"Right," the gangster behind the wheel replied. He looked down to the slumped form between the seats for a moment, then pulled smoothly away from the curb. There was nothing that could be done about the explosion of blood on the tan vehicle's door, but he rolled down the window to minimize most of the mess.

Wangara looked on, taken aback for a moment, but then she crawled forward and took the wounded man by the shoulders, cradling his head in her lap. He groaned, his forehead soaked with sweat. "Whatcha need, mate?" she asked Bolan.

"Keep him calm. Find something for him to bite down on so he doesn't tear up his tongue," Bolan said. He reached into his pocket and pulled out a folding multitool. He snapped it open, revealing a pair of needle-nosed pliers with wire cutters at the base. The slender tip of the pliers would be helpful for this, but first Bolan extended the slender length of an Allen wrench attachment, pushing it into the gunshot.

Luckily for Bolan's patient, the driver was deft as he steered the damaged van down the streets. The Allen wrench's tip tapped the base of the bullet and he withdrew the improvised probe. The Executioner upended the needle-nosed pliers and looked to Wangara, who still had her knapsack. She'd undone the strap and had placed the thick, leather shoulder pad between the injured man's teeth.

"That'll work?" she asked.

"Better than nothing," Bolan said. He leaned close to his patient, whispering, "Bite down, this is going to hurt."

"No shit," the triad man answered. He chomped hard on the shoulder pad, and Bolan reached in for the bullet. The man's eyes went wide, crossing with the pain. Fingers dug into the carpeting on the floor of the van as the multitool's tip pushed his injury slightly wider, the elastic skin and muscle spreading. Bolan closed the pliers on the base of the bullet. He tugged it back through the wound channel.

The man reached up, fingers clawing at Wangara's pants' cuff. He crushed the fabric, eyes shut tightly. The bullet was providing resistance, which meant that it had to have been a hollowpoint, the folded back petals of the tip making it far less aerodynamic. Bolan couldn't help it, and it took some effort to pull the bullet between his patient's ribs. He pulled the deformed slug until it was just under the skin. Using the tip of his combat knife, he opened the flesh to get the bullet out.

The man's grip loosened on Wangara's pants as Bolan pulled the slug free. The Executioner used his pocket light to examine the deformed bullet to see if it had fragmented. The blossom of lead and copper was a contiguous mass, leaving behind little, if any, shrapnel. He nodded to Wangara while tearing off the sleeves of his patient's shirt. He handed one to the young woman.

"Apply pressure to the wound," he told her. "Don't push hard, just firm. We don't want to aggravate any broken ribs."

She nodded.

"What's your name?" Bolan asked the driver.

The man nodded. "I'm Yin. He's Kue."

Bolan nodded. He gestured toward the unconscious man in the passenger seat. "Know this guy?"

"I'm not quite sure," Yin said.

"Be sure," Bolan told him. "Because I know I was hired by your people to do a job. If this guy is with the Black Rose Triad, that means I don't need either of you."

Yin swallowed. "I think I saw him with Frankie."

"Frankie?" Bolan asked.

Yin grimaced. "Frankie Law. He's one of the main Black Rose players in Darwin. Though why Frankie is getting in Big Brother Bobby's way…"

Bolan kept watching him. "What's sleeping beauty's name?"

"I don't know. I only saw him a couple of times. We don't get too chatty with the boys in Darwin. We'd only just come up here looking for her."

Bolan glanced back to Wangara in time to see her shudder.

"Why would Frankie send a hit squad after me and the girl?" Bolan pressed. "Especially one who didn't care if they killed one of the head man's group?"

Yin shrugged.

Kue moaned, his speech slurred by a combination of pain and blood loss. "Frankie wanted to be the one in charge. But when Big Brother Yeung was sent to oversee—"

"Kue!" Yin interjected.

"Aw, c'mon," Kue murmured. "This guy isn't stupid. He can figure out something just by who he was hired to kill."

"It's okay. You don't have to be specific," Bolan told

the wounded Kue. He searched his mental files for the
name Bobby Yeung, but the Chinese mobster was not of
sufficient rank to register in his memory. Neither was
Frankie Law. Unfortunately, the fluid nature of triad operations, given multiple organizations, of which the Black
Rose Triad was only one, and their traditional secrecy
helped them to stay below the radar of most law enforcement agencies, making it difficult for even Stony Man
Farm to keep track of their holdings in and out of main-
land China. However, with the names of the two top-tier
mobsters, Bolan had something to give to Kurtzman.
Maybe the Bear's cyber wizardry could pull up something
for the Executioner to work with.

Otherwise, Bolan was stuck in a reactionary role, having to navigate between two factions of a Chinese organized crime family. And knowing Eugene Waylon, it
wouldn't be long before another party entered this conflict on the Q.T. Waylon had informed Red of Bolan's
ruse, but if Bobby Yeung wasn't suspicious of his hired
gun, then the traitorous businessman couldn't have let the
triad boss know about his compromised meal ticket. It
seemed other people would be called in to take out the
Executioner, but on the sly. Waylon couldn't have a clue
about the fractured unity of the Chinese to take advantage
of Frankie Law's grab for power, because if any of the
Black Rose Triad had learned of Wade Augustyn's death,
Waylon would be forfeit himself, a useless aberration.

What had started as a simple and quick infiltration to
Hong Kong to eliminate a deadly assassin had pushed
Bolan into a maelstrom of conflict that he'd need every
ounce of skill to negotiate.

"We've got to talk to Yeung. We also can't sit still for long, because Law will know that his team failed," Bolan said. "Is there a safehouse available that Law doesn't know about?" Bolan nodded toward the unconscious wheelman. "Because I want to talk to his man."

Yin thought for a moment. "No. Not really, but I might be able to find someplace out of the way for us to park while you talk to him."

"That sounds good," Bolan said. He looked at the unconscious driver laying in the passenger seat well. A quick reexamination of Yin's face showed some subdued rage. Bolan assumed it was because of Kue's injury, due to the nervous glances he tossed in the rearview mirror toward his wounded buddy.

The attack was something that Yin took personally, and there was no doubt that Bobby Yeung would be equally irate over the trespass. For now, Kue's shooting and Bolan's deft treatment of the wound had forged a bond between the Executioner and the Black Rose soldiers. How long it would last? Bolan couldn't tell. Still, while the Executioner often leveled entire organized crime gangs, there was no way he could destroy every one of them. Nor did it seem probable to attempt such a complete razing operation. Instead, Bolan had found it easier to continue to form friendships and allegiances with lower-level fish, the men in the street who had enough of a conscience to develop loyalty to friends and avoid undue harm. Among that group, Bolan had fostered an edge to keep eyes inside enemy forces, be it among the Russian *mafiya* or South Seas pirates, though these disparate street toughs were mostly clueless about the big American who had shown them kindness and allegiance.

It was an act of mercy, sure, but it also fostered positive reinforcement for the less savage of his foes, instilling mercy in them and an aversion to even greater menaces who would interfere with their ordinary business. Bolan hoped that Yin would provide him with an in to the Black Rose Triad should this conflict end. But if the Chinese mobster decided that the Executioner was a threat, he would fall with a bullet to the head.

Bolan would have preferred to have another asset inside an opposition force. All of this flowed as a powerful undercurrent to his basic human decency in caring for the wounded Kue. He and Wangara continued to care for the gunshot victim as Yin drove along.

For now, mercy would be a stronger defense than all of Bolan's battle skills.

5

Bobby Yeung stretched and yawned. It had been a long night, not only finally getting into contact with the assassin from Hong Kong, but splitting up a major stealth shipment of heroin into the outback for eventual transport to their major markets across the world. In one night, Yeung had managed to process a month's worth of normal heroin transportation.

Australia's relatively sparse population for such a large continent enabled the Black Rose Triad's airplanes to slip in along unwatched stretches of coast and countryside, avoiding towns that would be curious about an anonymous cargo transport. With several tons of raw, unprocessed opium being flown in every three days along with slightly smaller amounts of already refined China White, Yeung knew he was sitting on a major gold mine.

Rather than depending on relatively vulnerable conventional shipping methods, the cargo planes tripled the speed at which the product was delivered. Splitting up the cut China White, Yeung's people loaded it onto smaller Lear jets that had been scheduled for legitimate flights to and from Australia, delayed only long enough to stop at the facility for its undisclosed cargo. From there, the charter jets spread out, not only through Southeast Asia, but to Hawaii to be transferred to the Americas or to Sri Lanka to disperse them through western Asia and Europe.

It was an ingenious clearinghouse, in the middle of one of the most remote areas on the planet. But, where it had proved a stealthy approach, it also meant that Yeung had his work cut out for him. It was fortunate that so far, the Black Rose's snakeheads had arranged for enough Chinese refugees to provide the bulk of the muscle power for the hard labor. Still, supervising everything on late-night shifts took energy.

He reached to his bedside table to take a sip of gin to relax his tired muscles when the small silver cell phone sitting next to it blurted out a few bars of a Tokyo pop ballad.

Yeung sighed and picked up the phone. "What's happening?"

"We've got the Wangara girl," Yin's voice said on the other end. Yeung couldn't miss the tension in his words.

"What else?" Yeung asked.

"Kue got shot," Yin added. "But thanks to the guy you hired he'll live."

Yeung took a deep breath. "What happened?"

"Five guys popped out of a van and tried to kill the girl," Yin stated. "Our own people."

"What!" Yeung exclaimed.

"They also shot at us. I ducked faster than Kue, and he took one in the upper chest. Our man did some emergency surgery on Kue, and he's getting better," Yin explained. "This was after your guy killed four of the five."

"What about the fifth?" Yeung asked.

"We're going to lean on him once we let him wake up," Yin said. "The assassin will make him talk. I think it's Frankie Law."

Yeung took a deep pull of gin, trying to douse the fires starting in his gut. It didn't work, the alcohol's warm, comfortable burn lost in his twisting bowels. "If Frankie tried to kill the girl—"

"He might be trying to make you look bad," Yin concluded.

"And the bosses, they don't like when we make mistakes. They tend to put us on the shelf, in tiny little cans of dog food," Yeung growled. "Find out if this fuck works for Law. I don't care if you leave him a stump, he spills his guts. And if Frankie is out for my ass, I want him to pay."

"Don't worry," Yin said. "I've seen the assassin at work. He's fucking amazing."

"I don't want Law amazed. I want him cold on a slab, got that?" Yeung snarled.

"Crystal clear," Yin replied.

"Until then, nobody else hears about this. Not the bosses, and especially not Frankie's people," Yeung said. "I don't want him to know we're coming after him. Is the assassin there?"

"Yeah," Yin said.

"Put him on," Yeung ordered.

"What's up?" Bolan asked.

"First, we need to know what to call you," Yeung said. "Sorry for prying."

"Call me Stone," Bolan answered.

"Good. I'm casting you, Stone," Yeung told him. "Find out who sent those mooks after you. If it's Frankie, then you're paid double for this trip."

"Double?" Bolan asked.

"You want more?" Yeung asked.

"I'd have taken him for normal price just for shooting at me," Bolan said.

"Consider this a bonus. I want Frankie, or whoever fucking sent that crew promptly serviced," Yeung ordered.

"You're asking this over an open phone line," Bolan warned.

"Fuck if I care. No one stabs me in the back," Yeung snapped. "I will not tolerate a war in my backyard. Yin will give you everything you need to tear the heart out of his operation."

"Gotcha," Bolan replied.

"Fail me—"

"If I do, I'll be dead already," Bolan interjected.

Yeung grunted in agreement. "Remember. Double pay. Prompt action."

"He's dead. He just doesn't know it," Bolan promised.

Yeung smiled. "Good hunting." He hung up and lay back on the bed. The word of the Western executioner soothed him like no amount of alcohol could. Bobby Yeung slept soundly.

ANG'S FIRST SENSATION after his long unconsciousness was the tightening of rope around his wrists and ankles. The hard floor was cold, and stones poked his chest and stomach as he lay on it.

"Do you speak English?" a man asked, kneeling beside

him. They were in an abandoned garage, the concrete floor cracked and broken in several places, dust and leaves littering the floor amid small rocks, blown in through excavated windows. Ang swallowed, looking into the Westerner's cold, hard eyes.

"Yes," Ang said. "It's why I was sent here."

The man shrugged, a loop of rope dangling from his hand. Ang tried to turn to see where the other end was, but he couldn't twist his head that far. The Executioner followed his gaze, and answered the unspoken question. "The other end of this noose is tied to your ankles."

With a flourish, Bolan pushed Ang's face up by the chin, stretching the noose roughly, fibrous hemp clawing along the triad man's face and hooking down under his jaw. When Bolan stopped pushing, the line between throat and ankles was drawn taut. In a few moments, Ang found it hard to breathe, and he bent his knees, creating slack.

"How long do you think you can keep your legs folded over like that?" Bolan asked.

"What?"

"See, in the old West, rather than bloody their weapons on a helpless prisoner, the tribes used to use a length of rope. They expended almost no effort, forcing their victims to strangle themselves. Eventually, muscle tension would make it so that they'd suffocate," Bolan explained.

Ang shuddered. The movement rasped the harsh rope across the skin of his throat. His legs cramped and he loosened them. He felt the strangling noose tighten over his windpipe. The gangster gurgled.

"I can let you go. You're only a driver. Throw yourself on Bobby Yeung's mercy, and all you'll walk off with is a few fractures and some rope burns," Bolan said. "If not—"

Ang sneered. "You're sick."

Bolan cuffed him in the back of the head. The impact relaxed Ang's legs again, and the sudden forward force induced a violent gag. Bile and spittle flowed over his lips as he bent again, giving himself just enough slack to breathe, but even then, he could feel his muscles yearning for release.

"If not, I'm not responsible. You'll simply hang yourself," Bolan told him. He flipped open a knife, the serrated blade on the pocket folder long and sharp, looking as if it could carve through the noose and end the grisly, self-induced suffocation with one swipe.

Bolan stood up, shaking out his stiff legs. Ang closed his eyes, trying not to emulate his captor's movements, feeling the twitching of muscle fibers in his thighs. Each twitch induced a jolt of tightness, cutting off his breath.

"You've got maybe twenty minutes before your leg muscles give out, and let's give it another five minutes for you to eventually run out of breath," Bolan added coldly and clinically. "In that time, it'll hurt like hell. Already your throat is raw. After ten more minutes, the hemp will flay the flesh from your neck, your blood soaking the ground under you."

"You wouldn't!" Ang exclaimed.

"I'm not doing it," Bolan reminded him. "You are. But hey, why give up Frankie Law? It's not like he's going to send someone to rescue you. It's not like he's going to argue for your continued existence before Bobby Yeung and the Black Rose high command."

"Wait! You already know. Why kill me?" Ang asked.

"Thing is, I don't know," Bolan said, stooping before him. "But are you just telling me what I want to hear? Or are you telling the truth? Because, frankly, you don't seem desperate enough yet."

"You'll smooth things over with Yeung?" Ang asked. "But you're—"

"White? Yeah. You're right. Why would any Westerner have any sway over a top triad boss?" Bolan asked. He stood up, stretching. The movement elicited another wave of twitches in Ang's muscles, his stomach tightening and rippling, those movements tugging painfully on his windpipe. His shirt collar felt damp. The rope had already chewed his skin enough to draw blood.

"Then again, why would Frankie send a van full of heavily armed men to take care of a little girl and two of Bobby Yeung's boys?" Bolan inquired. "Shotguns and pistols. And even then, I stepped through it all without a scratch, and you're the only survivor. It's as if I were death in a bottle, just there to be released for Bobby Yeung's whims."

Ang's eyes widened. "The assassin!"

Bolan nodded.

"And you'll take out Frankie?"

"You're giving him up?" Bolan asked.

"He'd kill me if he knew I was spilling everything!" Ang exclaimed. "But, with you on his case, I'll have a chance."

"Why should I protect you? After all, you didn't believe in me before," Bolan taunted.

"Frankie Law said for me to drive his boys to intercept

Bobby's men. I could tell, from the heat they were packing, it wasn't going to be a friendly meet," Ang explained.

"And you did it anyway?" Bolan said.

"Frankie's dangerous. Scary dangerous. That's how he got to be the stone-cold boss of Darwin."

Bolan thumbed his jaw, musing over the confession as Ang continued. "You let Frankie down, he saws your head off. He literally grabs a saw and takes it clean off."

"Pretty grisly," Bolan commented. He flicked his knife open, then shut.

"Please, it's getting harder to breathe," Ang whimpered. "I don't want to die."

"Few people do," Bolan replied.

Ang coughed, the spasm making his throat hurt. "At least not like this. Just stab me if you want me dead."

"So Frankie ordered this himself? Or someone else?"

"Frankie himself," Ang explained. "He told me to drive those boys to the meeting, keep the engine running, then get out as soon as everything settled down."

"He wanted the girl dead?"

"The girl. The white man with her. And Bobby Yeung's men," Ang stated. "I was told to come back with only his men, or not at all."

Bolan bent over Ang and sliced the rope. The man flattened out on the floor, coughing and breathing in deeply.

"I'll talk to Bobby Yeung. He won't come after you," Bolan told him. It was the truth in the Executioner's eyes. Not only would Frankie Law fall, but so would the Black Rose's boss in Australia. It was simply a matter of timing. Yeung wouldn't have the time for reprisals against Law's faithful, because once the renegade triad lieutenant and his private cadre were destroyed, Bolan would turn his attention to Yeung's side of this little civil war.

Ang's wrists were still tied behind his back. Bolan rolled him over and applied a damp cloth that soothed the roughed-up skin on his throat.

"Are you going to untie me?" Ang asked.

"The only reason Yin didn't beat you half to death was because I was going to get the information out of you," Bolan said. "I don't need to have him at my back. So, what are we going to do?"

Ang swallowed hard as the Executioner pulled the .44 Magnum Raging Bull. "Kill me?"

"Sounds good," Bolan told him. He fired the big Magnum twice, leaving Ang's ears ringing. "If you're lucky, Yin won't even survive to see that you lived after Law goes down." Bolan dropped a folding knife where Ang could reach it and walked out of the abandoned garage..

It took the triad wheelman a half hour to work up the courage to cut his bindings. He stared at the two deep craters, his right ear feeling funny from the muzzle-blast of the mighty .44 Magnum pistol.

Ang realized that he had dodged a bullet this time. He trembled, sincerely hoping that he wouldn't have to dodge any more for a long time.

YIN JERKED AS HE HEARD the thunder of a revolver. He glanced to Wangara, and then to Kue.

The assassin stepped out of the garage, casually replacing the two spent shells from his revolver, then snapping it shut. "You guys look like you're at a funeral," he said.

"You shot him?" Kue asked.

"Two .44s to the face. Want to see? You might want to watch your step," Bolan said in a taunting voice. He slid the revolver into its holster, letting his jacket drape over its butt. "Brain gets smelly, and it's hard to dig out of the tread on your shoes…"

Yin shook his head. Wangara looked as if she were about to throw up. Kue's bleary eyes looked the Executioner over. "He wasn't the one who shot me, man," he said.

"He was working for the guy who ordered you dead," Bolan answered. "Besides, you want to give up your floor space in the van for another body?"

Yin smirked. "Good riddance."

The Black Rose tough guy appeared to relish the opportunity to slip behind the wheel and drive Bolan where he needed to go.

Wangara edged closer to the garage door, and Bolan nodded to her. When she peeked in, she saw Ang, squirming on the broken concrete, two massive bullet craters just shy of his head. Wangara took a deep breath, then looked back to the Executioner as he helped load Kue into the back of the van. She put her hand over her face and evoked a tremor in her shoulders, walking slowly back to the vehicle. She wanted to hide the lack of horror on her face.

Bolan reached out and pulled her in.

"Get a good look?" he snarled.

She nodded numbly.

"Then you know not to rock the boat," Bolan said, letting her go. "Just sit down and shut up," he ordered.

She curled up in a corner in the back of the van, eyes

wide. Bolan acknowledged her acting with an upward turn of the corner of his mouth and a slight nod.

Wangara didn't like acting so frightened about the big stranger, but with just the right tone, he could elicit the reaction he wanted from her, and almost instantly bring her back to comfort. She considered her situation. She was certain this had to be the lone crusader that her grandfather had meant. He matched the description, and the battle inside the clothing store had all but proved that he was a fighting machine without peer.

The saving of one of the gangsters' lives with emergency surgery, and the recent mercy of not executing another mobster told her that this wasn't just some out-of-control killing machine. When he noticed doubt in her playing the role of frightened captive, he added just enough menace to his demeanor to get her to cringe. It was a delicate balancing act, because when he wanted to intimidate, he was a terror to behold. He did just enough to get her into the right frame of mind, without traumatizing her.

They hadn't had much time to confer in private, just the few minutes before the van loaded with gunmen showed up. However, in those few brief words he had won her over, despite his showy toughness for the other gangsters. That didn't mean he was soft, though. No one who wasn't a warrior through and through could have eliminated four heavily armed men in the space of a few seconds.

Then, only minutes later, he was able to save the life of a man. To kill in one heartbeat, and then to hold off death in the next, showed an amazing range of skill and dedication.

The most important thing was that he was the one keeping her alive.

From the sound of things, she thought he was going to destroy one member of the triad's leadership in order to curry favor with the ones in charge. With that task completed, Bobby Yeung, the smooth-voiced Chinese man who projected veiled threats toward her grandfather and the other tribe leaders of her home, wouldn't suspect the man as anything other than a trusted ally.

All the better to get in close and stab the gangster through an unprotected heart.

Wangara folded in on herself, lowering her head between her knees, catching some much-needed sleep.

6

Frankie Law was fuming. His boys were supposed to take down the Westerner who had been the Black Rose Triad's assassin as well as the girl he was brought in to capture. They hadn't reported in since noon, when they'd sighted the man. There had been a news report of a disturbance, and now, closing in on sunset, the rest of his inner cabal were growing tired, tense from being on guard all afternoon. Law could feel his own reserves of energy fading, waiting for the call from Bobby Yeung, but none had come.

He'd been left to sit and stew. For all Law knew, Yeung had assembled a small army of his own to charge on Darwin and burn his personal empire to the ground. He knew the triad frowned on disruptive civil wars, but they usually turned a blind eye to minor power struggles. Law didn't want his command of Darwin usurped by being made into a peripheral territory of Yeung's with his new facility. The Hong Kong native Yeung had made small rumbling noises about hating Australia, but that didn't keep him from dictating orders to Law who had been running in the streets of Darwin since he was a barefoot kid.

Law didn't want to become a second-stringer to Yeung. He whirled his Glock 19 in a circle by its trigger guard, spinning it like a propeller on his desktop. There was movement at the door and he snatched up the compact pistol, relaxing only when he saw that it was his man Ton.

"What's up?" Law asked.

"Just looking to see if we'd heard anything from the facility," Ton said. "Or from Hong Kong."

"Nothing. Bobby must be trying to keep this quiet," Law admitted. "If there's a ruckus here in town, it'll bring down the heat, not only from the authorities, but from the home base in Hong Kong."

"So no news is good news," Ton stated.

"Not exactly. The Westerner is still alive. And that man left four of our own dead in the middle of a street," Law replied. "We've pissed off a trained killer, and he's still on the loose in the city."

"The boys are on edge, boss. If we can't call in some relief soon, they'll burn out before the first shot is even fired," Ton said.

"I know that," Law grumbled. "Let half of them relax for an hour. Drinks, sandwiches, even women. But only an hour. The other half get to knock off in the next hour. If we put out the call for more men, it'll only bring us trouble. They'll know our movements."

"They can't be watching us that closely," Ton plied.

Law turned on the television, then cued the recording of the breaking news broadcast. Ambulances and police cars could be seen lining the street where four corpses were covered by tarps. Empty bullet casings glittered on the asphalt like copper snowflakes.

"It's headline news, Ton. We're fucked six ways to Sunday," Law snapped. "The Black Rose had the money and resources to tap our phones. Seems like we're girding for a shooting war."

"I had a couple of the kids send messages to people we have in the field," Ton admitted. "I didn't tell them not to use phones, but—"

"Hopefully they'll be quiet on the lines. What did you say?" Law interrupted.

"That we were expecting a shit storm, and we needed a few more guns to batten down the hatches," Ton stated. "Nobody's called yet."

There was a knock at the door.

"Sir, a new shift's come," one of Law's men said. "Another dozen guns."

Law breathed a sigh of relief, his shoulders unknotting. "Get the current shift to relax for a bit. You saved our asses."

Ton smiled.

That's when they heard the first thunderclap of a sawed-off shotgun blast in the distance.

THE EXECUTIONER CLUNG to the shadows in the labyrinthine alleys. A small shantytown had sprung up between the shops and their storehouses, and movement through the gnarled maze was slow and difficult, but with the throngs of Asian refugees, brought in by the snakeheads to provide an entire slave class to the Black Rose Triad, he was a phantom. Bolan's sunglasses, black leather jacket and dark shirt labeled him as bad news, not someone to be messed with.

Staying back, he spotted Law's Black Rose soldiers. They were clearly supposed to be on alert. Their faces were masks of stress-induced tension. Bulges under their jackets betrayed an arsenal of firepower, all meant to hold off either Bobby Yeung's men, or Bolan himself, under the guise of Wade Augustyn, the Black Rose's assassin. Bolan noted the despair present among his enemy, and he planned to add to it.

A sawed-off shotgun jutted under his shoulder, but the length of his leather jacket concealed it. He had scoped out Law's defenders, finding a small army of a dozen men, primed and ready. They'd been on alert for some time, however, and they were getting sloppy and tired. Half of them had already broken down, smoking and drinking coffee offered by the shanty residents, no longer paying much attention to movement in the shadows.

Bolan was about to make his move when he heard a small commotion.

A flock of newcomers was entering the maze, a group of fresh Black Rose gunmen. An examination of them from a distance showed that they had, at most, handguns tucked away under their jackets as they came in to bolster the exhausted crew. Bolan's advantage had been lessened, but not by much. The exhausted triad soldiers were the ones with the more effective weaponry, thus limiting the full potential of the recent arrivals.

One of the old guard turned and went into a storehouse, obviously to announce the arrival of a fresh shift. Bolan emerged from the shadows, maneuvering silently behind the new flock as they milled around the entrance of the storehouse. He slipped the ends of his improvised throwing knives from their forearm sheaths, their electrical tape handles providing him with a firm, tacky grip on them. He wouldn't throw them, not for his opening shot in this conflict.

The member of the old guard and the throng of new soldiers on hand had revealed to the Executioner the exact location of Frankie Law's office. The dozen men gathered near the entrance, waiting to accept the heavier weapons of their predecessors as they came off shift, but the changing of the guard would take a few minutes until Law gave the actual order to make the switch. With his knives hidden against his palms, Bolan closed on two of the Black Rose soldiers at the rear of the group as they talked and chuckled, feeling invincible now that they had strength in numbers.

Unfortunately, numbers only helped when the extra eyes were paying attention. As the pair scrambled for their weapons, Bolan lashed out with both blades, sinking the honed points into vulnerable flesh under ears. Their gurgling yelps as they tumbled, dying to the ground, drew the attention of their partners.

The sight of dying men froze those closest to the mortally wounded pair long enough for the Executioner to draw both his nine-inch butcher's knife and a Gerber LMF from their spots under his waistband. The heavy blade speared up and into the soft viscera of one Chinese gangster's belly, slashing through internal organs in one savage plunge of sharp-pointed steel. Bolan whipped the Gerber around, tearing across the eyes of another of the relief force before he brought it down in an ice-pick stab through the clavicle of a third man.

With the sudden and brutal attack on five of their own, the remaining men scrambled in a panic, reaching for handguns. Bolan spotted movement out of the corner of his eye and sidestepped, dragging the opponent he'd blinded in front of him as a shield. The maneuver saved Bolan from being struck by a quartet of buckshot pellets as one of the old guard's shotguns blasted at him. Bolan's human shield sputtered, his heart torn apart by the four .36-caliber pellets tearing through it.

The Executioner heard more screams from behind him. The Black Rose relief team was taking injuries from the spreading buckshot, the remainder of the initial shotgun blast that had killed the blinded triad gangster. Bolan snapped his own shotgun out to its full length on an improvised sling, safety snicking off. His return fire knocked the Black Rose shotgunner off his feet, as he took the Executioner's well-aimed shot in his face and upper chest. The Chinese scattergunner flopped back, a cloud of misty blood and pulverized tissue floating in the air from the brutal blast.

One of the mobsters got his 9 mm pistol out and thrust it at Bolan, but the Executioner simply whirled, batting the handgun aside with the barrel of his 12-gauge. A snap-kick lashed up between the hatchet man's legs, the force of the blow lifting the smaller man off his feet and dropping him on his face. A second gunner was bringing his pistol to bear when Bolan racked the shotgun and fired again, buckshot hitting breastbone. Pellets struck flesh and spiraled, ricocheting off bone and one another, tunneling and severing blood vessels in their wake. The Black Rose shooter's torso became a blast crater as the shotgun smashed him deeply. Blood vomited from his lips as he tumbled back across a third gunner still in middraw. His lifeless body pinned his living compatriot, buying Bolan time to turn his attention to other opponents.

Movement caught the Executioner's attention and he surged against another of the fresh shift, knocking him back with a hard shoulder block. Bolan's forward momentum carried both men through the doorway as a machine pistol chattered. Two men wailed as stray rounds burned through their chests as a too-tired guard tried to cut down Bolan. The Black Rose reinforcements had been devastated not only by Bolan's efforts, but by the stray fire of their own allies. The Executioner didn't have an estimation of who was down for the count, but he wasn't going to waste precious moments considering incomplete intelligence when he was under fire.

Bolan clamped his left hand over his tackle dummy's face. Shoving hard he heard the back of the triad gunman's head crack on the hard ground. He followed up, middle knuckle jutting in front of a fist to form a point that crashed into the soft flesh under his foe's ear. The impact sent a shock wave through the man's head, sending him into seizures. The Executioner rose from the stunned man, pulling a Glock from his waistband.

Half turning, he saw the machine-pistol gunner fill the doorway. Bolan's Glock cracked twice, punching 9 mm bullets through the man's sternum before the scattergunner could lock on to him. The deadly Parabellum rounds spilled the gunman out into the alley.

The stunned triad man sat up, clawing for a revolver in his pocket. Bolan whirled and lashed his heel against the

gangster's jaw, bone crunching under the force of his kick.
The Black Rose mobster flopped limply to the ground.
Bolan took a step back, working the pump on his shotgun
by jamming it in the crook of his elbow and sawing it back
and forth. The clack-clack of the pump was audible as the
fusillade of enemy fire died down. Three men swung
around, looking to get the drop on Bolan, unaware that the
rack of the shotgun was as much bait as reloading his
weapon.

Drawn into the Executioner's line of sight, they were
sitting ducks as Bolan shoved his weapon to full extension and triggered a 12-gauge blast of devastation into the
trio. One man folded, clutching his ruined guts, while another man screamed as pellets tore across his arm and side.
The Executioner then stiff-armed his Glock and tapped
out a 9 mm round through the center of the unwounded
mobster's face. The bullet entered the bridge of the man's
nose and exited in a spray of brains and blood through the
base of his skull. Bolan shifted his aim to the triad gunner he'd only winged, burning off three more rapid 9 mm
rounds into his upper chest.

Bolan immediately hit the deck, hearing curses in Chinese, and understanding the order to fire coming from inside the building. Bullets tore at the brick, slugs smashing
through the mortar. Chips of shattered brick spit through
divots blown through the wall. The Black Rose gunmen
weren't going to expose themselves to the tall, dark wraith's
withering return fire again. Slithering across the ground
on his elbows and knees, the Executioner crawled to a position where he could draw the .44 Magnum Raging Bull.
The mighty revolver rested in his big hand easily, and

when a quartet of bricks gave way to a shotgun blast, opening a portal through the heavily abused wall, Bolan could see a triad soldier working the slide on his scattergun.

The Raging Bull snorted, its 240-grain payload spitting through the gap blown by the shotgunner. The hollowpoint round caught the Chinese gangster on the point of his chin, splintering his mandible. The gaping hole that used to be the mobster's lower face spewed forth a torrent of gore and his head flopped. The devastating effect of Bolan's revolver had raised a chorus of dismayed cries as they watched the horrific demise of their leader.

The Executioner capitalized on their state of shock, stepping back by the doorway and hammering off another blast that tore the top off another Black Rose gunman's head. The dying man's machine pistol hit the ground. The soldier sagged across the path of two of his allies who let loose a cry of panic as they stared at their fallen partners. Bolan calmed the duo with a pair of 9 mm rounds from his confiscated Glock.

Four more cut from their numbers, the Black Rose gunmen broke and ran, fleeing from the entrance to Frankie Law's offices, rather than continue to tempt fate against a man who had slaughtered a dozen opponents despite being surrounded and outgunned.

Bolan glanced at the wall the combined triad gunfire had torn through. Several gaping holes had been blasted by shotguns and machine pistols firing at close range. A half-dozen weapons had been emptied, enough to create the hole Bolan had shot through. They had wasted their ammunition in a wild attempt to put him down.

The Executioner's audacity and skill had turned the tables, leaving the superior force in a state of disarray.

THE GUNFIRE OUTSIDE ROSE to a crescendo, freezing Law at his desk. Then in the space of four rapid gunshots, it was over outside. Law's heart hammered in his chest as he snatched up the Glock 19.

Ton was at the window, his eyes wide in shock.

"What's happening?" Law asked.

"They're running," Ton muttered.

"What?" Law pressed.

"They're running. He just popped up like some kind of nightmare," Ton said louder. He had his Desert Eagle in his trembling hand. "He popped up and our people started dying, and when they shot him he didn't die and he just—"

"Shut up," Law growled. "Come on. Out the back."

Ton backed away from the window, the massive pistol in his hand trembling. "They couldn't bloody kill him—"

"Ton, either move your ass or I'm leaving you!" Law snapped.

Ton looked up numbly. "It won't matter. It won't fucking matter."

Law spit on the floor and spun, heading toward the hall. He spotted a shadow splayed across the wall, coming up the steps, but he held his fire. Instead, he tore off toward the fire escape. Law hit the door and slammed his shoulder into it, shoving it open. Behind him, he heard Ton scream. He was calling to his ancestors for forgiveness, praying they accept him into their arms.

Ton's Desert Eagle thundered in the confines of the tiny office, but instead of return fire, Law heard the loud crack of bones and Ton's wail of agony. Law threw himself down the stairs, landing with the rattle of his shoes on metal. He raced to the next flight of metal steps and leaped when he was halfway down them, landing on the ground just as he heard the door he'd escaped through slam wide open.

Law didn't look back. He knew if he paused for even a moment, Ton's words that the man on his heels was unstoppable would be proved true. He lowered his head and dug in, pulling every ounce of speed from his legs. His muscles burned as he dashed wildly toward his Mercedes. Law stabbed his hand into his pocket, tugging out the keys even as he charged along, Glock gripped tightly in his fist.

Law thumbed the remote lock button on his key chain, relieved when he heard the sound of his car receiving the signal to unlock. He slammed against the side of the car, fingers fumbling for the door latch, but with his hands occupied by the keys and the pistol, it took time. Finally he hooked the latch, pulling the door open. He ducked into the car seat, feeling the shock wave of a massive slug slamming into a rear window, blowing it to smithereens.

Law lurched behind the wheel, ducking as a bullet tore through the air over his head. He speared the key against the steering wheel base, poking the plastic three or four times before the end of the key ratcheted into the lock. He twisted it, shoving his hand against the gas. The engine revved for a few moments before Law realized that he needed to shift the gear out of Park. The car shot forward, plowing through boxes as another heavy slug smashed against the car.

"Please, please, please," he murmured as the Mercedes sped into the street. It jolted as he clipped the rear fender of a compact car, but the gunfire of his pursuer stopped.

Law sat up, adjusting so that he could drive normally instead of half hanging out the driver's door. He glanced back in time to see a man in black rushing toward the back of the car. Stomping the gas, the triad gangster cranked the wheel, soaring into traffic. Something hard smashed the rear windshield.

Law saw a hole had been punched through the glass by a massive gun. The assassin hung on through the hole. Law screamed and jammed his foot to the floorboards, weaving between cars. The front end of his Mercedes bounced off the side of a panel van, and he wrestled to control it, aiming straight ahead. In his side mirror, he could see the man as he hung on for dear life.

Law reached for the Glock 19 and twisted, aiming toward the assassin. Before he could pull the trigger and pump a 9 mm round through the man's face, the Mercedes jerked to a halt. The air bag exploded in Law's face as he was hurled forward. The Glock was knocked out of his hand, and his world was filled with a cloud of white, the nylon of the air bag shell smothering his face for a moment.

He slumped back, seeing the bag deflate, seeing the wrinkled, crumpled hood popped and steam pouring out of the engine block.

Law clawed at the door, tugging at the release latch. The door popped open, but as he lurched out of his seat, the door slammed back shut, banging against his forehead. Stunned, he could see the assassin, his tanned face covered with blood. He leveled two huge weapons at Law.

"Don't go for the Glock," Bolan growled.

Law froze.

"Bobby Yeung thinks I'm going to kill you," Bolan informed him. "It's your choice whether I do that job or not."

Law shuddered, terrified. "Why not?"

The Desert Eagle and the Raging Bull were unwavering, two huge barrels looming as if they were train tunnels, locking Law's attention. He didn't dare look at the blood-spattered monster behind the two guns, because he was certain that the man was even more frightening than two Magnum cannons leveled at his face.

Law focused on the guns. "What do I need to do?" he asked.

"Play dead for a few days. Your office is going up in flames, and your lackey's corpse will serve as good as yours until it's time to come out of hiding," Bolan said.

"How will I know?" Law asked.

"When Yeung's facility is destroyed," Bolan answered. "The facility burns to the ground, and so does Bobby Yeung. He goes down, you come back to life but you do business a new way."

Law dared to look at the assassin. "What way?" he asked, confused.

"You do right by your people. No slavery. No hurting anyone not in the business. No drugs to kids, no abusing women. Steal all you want, run crooked gambling, run your whores clean, safe, happy and healthy with respect. I hear about one dead body showing up in Darwin, and it stinks of triad, you better tell me it's another triad when I come down on your neck, or put a noose around your own neck and take a long walk off a short chair," Bolan told him. "Clean up or die. Simple."

"How do I clean up? What if the bosses back home want more?" Law asked.

"Then you tell me," Bolan said. He gave the mob boss a number. "I'll set them straight or burn them down."

Law nodded, his eyes cast toward his lap. "Okay," he said quietly.

"Triad was once a force for justice in China. You can start being right. You've got a corrupt politician in your line of sight. Go for him and make all the money you can. Someone preys on your people, you back him off or put him in the ground. Be just or be dead. Simple choice," the Executioner pronounced. "Have you made your choice?"

"Yes," Law answered, trembling. "I want to live."

"Then live," Bolan said. He lowered the guns. "When you bury your boy, tell him thanks for the Desert Eagle."

Law took a moment to glance up, and noticed the tall dark shape fading away down the street, a shadow blending into the crowd. He knew death had passed on him this day. He heard the wail of fire engines in the distance, racing to put out his flaming offices.

7

Red was forthcoming with a hip holster for the confiscated Desert Eagle and spare magazines. Bolan had traded in the Raging Bull, which would be rebarreled so the sporting goods store owner could make the gun involved in the deaths of several Black Rose soldiers disappear for good. The .44 Magnum ammo would go into the Desert Eagle magazines as easily as into a revolver cylinder. The big pistol was a familiar tool for the Executioner, and his intimate knowledge of the weapon would give him an increased edge.

Bolan also traded in the sawed-off shotgun, keeping a superior tool, a Heckler & Koch MP-5 he'd captured from one of Frankie Law's soldiers. The shotgun would be rebarreled and given a proper stock to turn it back into a sporting or home defense tool. Stockless, it was worthless for anything in untrained hands. Only Bolan's great physical strength and improvised sling had made it useful along with his experience and skill.

Yin was impressed at the efficiency of Bolan's support, not knowing it was just a last-minute alliance formed between the Executioner and Red. All he knew was that the man he knew as Stone had walked in with a sack full of triad discards, and walked out with all the necessities for his latest pickups.

Bolan climbed into the passenger seat of a BMW SUV he had taken from Frankie Law's own lot. Yin sat behind the wheel.

Kue was recuperating in a hotel that Bobby Yeung had arranged, leaving Arana Wangara alone in the backseat of the powerful luxury wagon. The BMW was less conspicuous than a shot-up van, and more comfortable for the trio of passengers with better air-conditioning and softer seats.

Bolan felt a weight off his conscience. For now, Ang was out of the picture, no longer in danger while Frankie Law was laid low under Bolan's threat. The Executioner's intimidation would buy him some breathing room, but his experience told him he couldn't trust Law for long. He gave Red his cell number and asked the black marketeer to keep an ear out for any massive rearming efforts. Red had already heard that Law was asking for crates of ammunition and brush-hunting camouflage. Bolan knew that Law was not going to allow Bobby Yeung's insult to go unchallenged, and with the Executioner's proclamation that the facility would fall, the seed was planted that all of Law's enemies would be in one spot. Bolan had given him that bait, in order to draw Law's remaining organized forces right into his sights. Since Law was going to try to take care of business with Yeung, Bolan was pleased to have at least a three-way conflict stoked by his actions.

Then there was Eugene Waylon. Kurtzman had finally cracked Augustyn's encryptions, and had picked up on a phone call stating that Waylon was in communication with a group of men in transit to Darwin by private charter. Bolan was under no delusion that these men were anything but highly trained fighting men, the type recruited by the assassin Augustyn to back his play on particularly spectacular, paramilitary eliminations. Kurtzman had listed eight men on the charter flight, each carrying impressive amounts of luggage. Those men, that heavily armed, would push Bolan to his limits while he was occupied with the other teams. He needed to give himself an edge beyond what he'd already assembled in weapons and vehicles.

Bolan had the MP-5 and the Desert Eagle. From Red he'd received an accurate, light-triggered 9 mm Walther P-99 and a sniper rifle. His arsenal would give Bolan a chance to turn the tide on any ambush set up by Waylon's killers.

The switch to the BMW would also help. The SUV was a touring vehicle, something that people on holiday would use. The chassis of the SUV was heavier and tougher than the van, and Bolan could tell by the wagon's handling that it had been bulked up with a layer of armor, as befitting a triad crew wagon. Exploring the door, he found a small compartment, large enough for a collapsed MP-5 or a couple of kilogram packages of heroin. The back of the compartment was a reinforced sheet of steel, making the door weigh heavier. The glass itself was thick, causing refraction that informed Bolan of its bulletproof properties.

The Executioner was realistic. An armored SUV wasn't going to provide more than a few moments of protection. The rolled steel might last longer, but the shatter-resistant glass would eventually cave in under an assault by military caliber weaponry. The armoring necessary to completely protect from even a light machine gun would make the SUV a slow, sluggish tank, guzzling gas, rendering it useless for long-range travel. The brief amount of protection would bounce handgun fire, and fend off an attack long enough to hit the gas and get the hell out of Dodge.

"You promised Booby Frankie's head," Yin spoke up.

Bolan looked at him. "A cooked fifteen pounds of meat and bone? You want to sit with that for a few hundred miles?"

Yin wrinkled his nose at the thought. "All charred, there'd be no way for the boss to identify it anyway, right?"

"Not unless he had Frankie's dental records. All the skin had peeled off his skull," Bolan answered.

"Christ, you don't do anything halfway, Stone." Yin sighed.

"I only go as far as I have to. It's up to my targets to decide how hard they want to die," Bolan replied. "Pull over and let's top off the tank. Use this card."

Yin nodded, taking the credit card from Bolan. The Executioner had acquired the card from Eugene Waylon. It was one of Wade Augustyn's cards. He knew the businessman would be alerted to the purchase, and Waylon would be able to predict Bolan's path toward the facility. That information would be relayed to the death squad flying into Darwin, and help them close in on him. Bolan looked back to Wangara, free to speak now that Yin was busy.

"That card belongs to the assassin I took the identity of,"

Bolan informed her. "I'm leaving a trail for his people to follow me and find me. Sometime before we hit Alice Springs, there is going to be a group of six to eight men attacking us, all heavily armed, and out to kill me. At the first sign of trouble, I want you to hug the floorboards. If we've stopped, crawl away. I'll attract all the attention toward me."

"What'll I do if they kill you?" the young woman asked.

"Hide. Stay out of sight," Bolan said. He handed her a business card. "Call that number. My people will pick you up and protect you, no matter what."

"Why can't you call them in now?" she pressed.

"I'm too far away from my support teams," Bolan said, watching Yin. "And slowing the schedule will only snarl things up when Law and Yeung go at it."

"You let Law live?" she said, surprised.

"I'm bringing the Black Rose elements together so I can clean them out," Bolan replied. "Your people will never be troubled by the triad again."

"You can clean them out," Wangara repeated. "By yourself?"

Bolan gave her a reassuring smile. "It's what I do. Now quiet. Yin's coming back."

She pursed her lips, big brown eyes swiveling fearfully toward the Chinese gangster.

"Why's she so nervous?" Yin asked as he entered the car.

"I told her who'd take over if I couldn't get her grandfather's location out of her on my own," Bolan said with a vicious snarl.

Wangara tensed as Yin chuckled. "Don't worry, girlie. I'll be gentle."

Wangara glared at Bolan, who winked at her. She settled back into her nervous shifting. Bolan wished he didn't have to keep yanking her around emotionally, and promised himself that he'd do what he could to soothe whatever psychological damage he'd caused. He just needed to keep her alive long enough for that to happen.

Yin pulled out of the gas station, heading for Alice Springs, where Bolan and Bobby Yeung would meet face-to-face to discuss the growing pile of corpses.

FRANKIE LAW STUFFED the money into the coroner assistant's hand, seething with rage as he walked over to the steel table where Ton lay. Law tried to deny the tears burning at the corners of his eyes, looking at the young man, flesh blackened and flaking off, bits dropping like snow to the polished metal. Ton's right arm was twisted horrifically, and there was a hole through his throat, the top of his skull having erupted with a nearly half-inch hole rising atop a funnel of cracked bone.

Law was tempted to touch the dead man's cheek, his heart aching. Ton had been more than a lieutenant to the Black Rose boss, and he couldn't believe such a beautiful face had been charred to a blackened husk, ashes sloughing off bone and charred flesh.

"You can't touch him," the assistant told Law.

"I know," Law answered, his throat tight and constricted. "I know."

Law's phone warbled and he plucked it out. "I'm busy."

It was Pei, another of Law's lieutenants. Unlike Ton, however, Pei had never been Law's lover. "I'm sorry, but I managed to call in some help from the snakeheads.

We've got at least twenty more bodies. We'll make Bobby and that big scary bastard pay."

Law looked down at Ton, remembering how he had snapped and run, leaving the young man behind. His anger at Yeung and his assassin was shadowed by his shame at abandoning Ton. He tried to explain it away as the contagious terror emanating off his lover, but the truth was, the sound of the war had put him on edge. He'd been broken, Ton's terror simply being the icing on the cake.

He'd lost his strength, and in the eyes of the Black Rose Triad, that would be his death. The triad didn't care who Law slept with, male or female, as long as he was strong enough to fight like a man. Breaking and running like a coward was not tolerated.

"You're right," Law said. "I'll be at the front of this. I'll pull Yeung's heart out of his chest."

EUGENE WAYLON UNTENSED the moment he heard the alert chime on his computer. The fool had used Augustyn's credit card in Australia. He turned on the screen and clicked on the alert icon. The man who'd assassinated his meal ticket had just stopped at an Australian gas station on a major road on the south side of Darwin. He called up his map and saw that the road was on a highway headed deep into the outback.

He hit the speed dial on his cell phone. Garret Victor picked up on the first ring.

"What's up?" Victor asked.

"Where are you right now?" Waylon asked.

"We just landed. No trouble with the charter you got

for us," Victor answered. "The rentals are perfect. Two Land Rovers."

"You have a map of Darwin with you?" Waylon asked.

"You've got a location?" Victor inquired. Waylon heard the mercenary rustle through something on the other end.

Waylon read off the address of the gas station. "He just used the card fifteen minutes ago, so he's barely just left the city limits."

"He used the credit card you gave him to load up on gasoline?" Victor asked. "He's actually not too far away, say a half an hour. But this is strange."

"Why?" Waylon inquired.

"This guy is using Augustyn's card, right? Why? He was able to get to Hong Kong on his own," Victor mused aloud.

"I'm hiring you to kill him," Waylon stated. "Be a good little soldier."

"Good soldiers finish the job, not walk right into an ambush," Victor returned. "If this guy was good enough to take out Wade, then he's no rank amateur. He wouldn't make a stupid mistake like broadcasting his position."

"Ambush," Waylon murmured. He heard Victor speaking, as if he were on the other side of a mile of cotton. "What's wrong?"

"I'm putting one of my people on this. He's going to do some quick research," Victor told him. "We'll take this bastard down, but we're all walking home from this fight."

"You doubled the size of your team. What else could you want?" Waylon asked.

"Fuck," Victor snarled.

The phone went dead. Waylon's ears burned and he

quickly dialed again. "Who the fuck do you think you are, Garrett?"

"You just gave away my troop strength on an open line, damn it," Victor answered. "Piss off!"

The phone went dead yet again.

Waylon was on speed dial in a heartbeat. "Do you think I'm stupid? These phones have the best encryption codes on the planet. No one can listen to us!" he shouted.

Waylon listened for a moment, waiting for an answer. All he heard was a click.

In frustration, the businessman hurled the cell phone against the wall, watching its shell shatter, electronic components exploding and spraying across the top of his desk. He took a deep breath and ran his fingers through his graying hair, trying to control the frustration boiling through his veins. The phone was replaceable. He wasn't sure, though, that Victor and his team would continue their operation, not the way that they were stonewalling him.

His computer chimed and he pulled up an e-mail from an unknown location. Waylon scanned it through his virus checker and found it clean. He opened it, and read two simple lines. "Everything can be broken, Eugene. How do you think Wade ended up dead?"

Waylon nodded, chewing his lower lip. "Then how do we keep in touch?" he typed.

Victor's e-mail response took a minute. "On the phones. But no more details about us. Operational security, which I admit to having broken by stating my location. Stay calm, and we'll get the job done. Purge these e-mails."

Waylon trashed everything and ran his computer's power tools, scrubbing every trace of the e-mails off his hard drive. Paranoia tensed his shoulders again, knotting his muscles. Waylon poured himself a tumbler full of brandy, downing it all in one gulp. The alcohol did nothing to ease his wired nerves. He was glad for the brief respite he had when he considered that he had Wade's killer right where he wanted him.

Poking at the chip set that gave his phone its encryption, he fought against the returning paranoia whose jaws opened wide to swallow him whole. He opened a drawer and put a .45 pistol on the blotter in front of him.

THOUSANDS OF MILES AWAY, in a small farm nestled under the Blue Ridge Mountains, Aaron Kurtzman sat at a messy computer station, collating data from the telephone call he'd just intercepted. He was glad that he wasn't needed for anything else at the moment, because he would be able to give Mack Bolan all the support he needed.

"Hunt, I need you to run rental records in Darwin, Australia, for two Land Rovers rented at the same time, and where they were delivered. It'll probably be a private airport, or one that handles multiple private charters," Kurtzman requested. "Eugene Waylon made the arrangements, so, Akira, flag those accounts and see if any of Augustyn's old fronts were used to get the Rovers. The two of you work toward each other."

Huntington Wethers nodded. "I'm on it."

Akira Tokaido grinned and inserted his earbuds, fingers blazing across his keyboard.

"Carmen?" Kurtzman began.

"I'm checking American ex-military men with the name Garrett who have gone into independent contracting in the South Pacific," Carmen Delahunt answered.

"Read my mind," Kurtzman replied. "I'll be checking our wanted lists to see if I can get any hits on this guy and his crew. Striker will need all the info we can find, so once you locate those Land Rovers, Hunt, get some satellite imagery on them so we can track them."

"Actually, if Hunt can scare up the VIN numbers," Tokaido began, "I might be able to pull up their GPS units and track them that way. A rich guy like Waylon would be fronting some major cash for his mercs, so he'd go with the best off-roaders he could arrange, and of late, most of those rentals come with GPS security packages, so that the agencies won't lose them in the middle of nowhere."

"I want belt and suspenders on this," Kurtzman replied. "Garrett seemed to be getting paranoid at the end of that first call, and he confirmed it with the two subsequent hang-ups."

"There's nothing on our e-mail filters to Waylon," Delahunt mentioned. "That means we're working in the dark if Waylon got smart and cleared his cache."

"I'll get to work monitoring the server he got the mail through. Mail portals will retain the footprints of any e-mails sent to Waylon, so we can pick those up," Wethers stated.

"Let's get on it," Kurtzman replied.

GARRETT VICTOR TOSSED a roll of pound notes to Lucenzo. "You know the deal."

Lucenzo winked. "Two bikes, bought legal. Gotcha."

Lucenzo took off with Talarico. The two little Italians were the best motorcyclists in Victor's acquaintance, and they would prove to be vital advance scouts when it came to tracking down the mysterious assassin. Since the bikes would be off Waylon's payroll, whoever their mysterious quarry was working with wouldn't be able to trace them so easily. Victor went to work loading his gear into the back of one of the SUVs.

Stoffer stared at his laptop intensely.

"What've you got?" Victor asked.

"I hacked the digital video the gas station was using for a security camera. Found the vehicle we're watching out for. It's a black BMW SUV," Stoffer replied. "Our man didn't get out, he had one of the local mooks fill her up and pay for the gas. Here." Victor looked closely. Sure enough, it was just another generic Chinese organized crime soldier, packing heat under his jacket.

"Let me see the BMW again," Victor said.

"I got a plate, and there's someone in the backseat, but it's too small to be anyone we'd have to worry about," Stoffer said.

Victor looked in the car and saw a scrawny young woman.

"Okay, so she's probably not a combatant," Victor said. "Good work hacking their security."

"Fuck, that's why you've got me on the team," Stoffer answered. "I'm good and fast."

Stoffer plugged his laptop's power cord into the Toyota's charger, then handed another cord to Victor. "Stick this into the data port under the dash. I'm going to kill the GPS on this ride."

"I was just going to ask you to do that," Victor replied. "You going to do the same for the other?"

"Actually, I'm going to clone ours to theirs," Stoffer said. "After all, that's why you hired Brendan, right? He's good for nothing but rolling wildly around the countryside."

"Smart," Victor stated. "This way if someone has managed to hack on to us, they'll think we're farther away than we really are."

Victor's phone chirped. "Talk to me, Lucenzo."

"Got the bikes. Heading off to the station and will follow their projected course to Alice Springs," Lucenzo announced. "Got a description?"

"Black BMW SUV," Victor answered. He read off the license plate that Stoffer had picked up.

"Bee-fucking-you-tee-full," Lucenzo quipped. "I'll see how hard that ride is."

"Judging by the gas mileage, it's heavily armored, more than they've got with them," Stoffer offered.

"Heard that, Luc?" Victor asked. "Lay eyes only. Any fire, and what he doesn't kill, I will. Got that, soldier?"

"Aye-aye, sir!" Lucenzo answered. Victor heard the bike snarl to life on the other end of the phone, then the signal cut out.

"If I ever get that macho stupid, shoot me in the head," Stoffer said.

"If you do get that stupid, shooting you in the head wouldn't do shit," Victor responded.

Stoffer chuckled.

"All right, people, let's move out! This day's not getting any fucking longer! We've got a job to kill," Victor shouted.

8

The Executioner had long been an advocate of advanced intelligence, and a good support base. However, there were times when the soldier simply had to play things by ear. All he had from Kurtzman were a few hints as to what was going on. Everything else was going to have to come from his experience on the ground. Riding shotgun as Yin drove, he pretended to sleep while he kept his eye on the side mirror. His body was stilled to a Zenlike calm, rejuvenating for his sore, battle-tested muscles. He was alert and ready, his hands never far from the MP-5 in its door compartment, or the Desert Eagle and Walther in their holsters.

The BMW SUV chugged along the road, the Australian countryside spinning past the window. Bolan was certain the mercenaries Eugene Waylon hired weren't going to be able to use a helicopter to trail him—the distances they needed to cross and the fuel costs would be prohibitive. Bolan also knew that any mercenary worth his salt would have plans he'd hide from his employer. He considered the conversation that Kurtzman had listened in on, betraying the merc's knowledge of possible phone tapping.

There were a couple of ways Bolan would shadow an opponent for long stretches on a highway. One of them was a team of motorcycles. It was a likely scenario simply because of the ease of picking up a bike and the relative compactness of the vehicle. A good biker could trail someone for miles, using cars for cover, hiding behind them and drifting along. Most people wouldn't pay much attention to a biker even if he did pop out into the open.

Kurtzman hadn't reported anything about the mercenaries using bikes, but he had pointed out, in text messages, that the team had split up, according to a satellite photo. The Farm had managed to get a lock on their GPS trackers, but when the GPS movements didn't match the movement of the second vehicle, Bolan was alerted that the opposition was well prepared. They'd had the technical know-how to remove the GPS device and plant it in the second vehicle. Having traveled over a hundred miles, the mercenaries' driver had managed to elude the satellite camera and alter their trucks' appearance as well.

Communicating with the Farm by text messaging kept Yin in the dark about the nature of Bolan's intel, especially since the Executioner was able to pass it off as keeping in touch with his support back in Hong Kong. Since the triad wanted to maintain some plausible deniability, Yeung had ordered Yin to give the assassin his space.

"I spotted something," Yin said, giving Bolan a light tap on the shoulder so as not to awaken Wangara from her sleep in the backseat. She had curled up, a low purr of a snore escaping her as she enjoyed the first truly restful slumber she'd had in days.

Bolan had seen it, too, a solitary motorcyclist, hanging far back, staying behind other cars, only visible for brief glimpses. Still, it was a presence that gnawed at the Executioner's combat senses. "Me, too," he told Yin.

"Considering that this is a long road and the next town isn't for another hundred miles, I'm wondering why he's zipping around without any serious baggage," Yin spoke up.

"The bike looks too clean for someone who regularly travels long-distance," Bolan added, slouched in his seat.

"You noticed that, too?" Yin asked. "You are good. I thought you were sound asleep."

"Advance scouts, most likely," Bolan said, ignoring the compliment. "I think they're just after me, though, not you."

"What makes you say that?" Yin asked.

Bolan glared at him. "I have a lot of people who'd like to kill me if they could pin me down. Probably the U.S. government."

"Kill, or arrest?" Yin quizzed.

"Kill," Bolan answered. "They owe me too much to put me in a jail. This is a black bag team that's been dogging me for the past few months."

Yin tensed. "You're sure?"

"Frankie Law is a crispy critter, and Bobby Yeung needs me to kill her granddad and a bunch of his buddies," Bolan responded. "And no one else I've touched is smart enough or good enough to track me down."

"I'll handle them. Just keep your wits. I need you to drive, and watch out for any tails."

"You think the biker will try anything?" Yin asked.

"No. His ride doesn't have any compartments large enough to hide a submachine gun. There aren't any concealable handguns that can hurt this baby," Bolan replied. "The real firepower will be in another truck like this one, along with four or five shooters with rifles and maybe a grenade launcher or two."

Yin's eyes danced to the mirror. "He's falling back. I caught sight of him."

"He pressed something on his throat, which means he's in communication with the rest of his team," Bolan explained. "They've got us cold. But they don't know we know they're on to us."

Yin's knuckles whitened on the steering wheel. "So we know where they are, but so what?"

"Knowledge is power," Bolan stated. "We'll just pull them into a trap."

"You, me and an unarmed prisoner against an American government team?" Yin asked, nodding toward the sleeping teenager.

Bolan nodded. "Yeah. They're dead."

Yin looked dubious, but the Executioner had played his role of cocky assassin to the hilt. Bolan's confidence was infectious, and the young triad driver was ready to listen to any suggestions. Bolan could see that if he said all they needed were sharpened spoons, Yin would agree the enemy could be taken. Fortunately, Bolan's strategy didn't require anything so reckless and suicidal, and the experiences of the past day cemented Yin's respect for the tall warrior and his planning abilities.

"So where should we do this?" Yin asked.

Bolan looked at the roadside sign, stating that the town of Whiterock, population 150, was eighty kilometers ahead. "Sometime after we hit Whiterock. We'll stop for something to eat, and we'll pump some more gas. I'll take the time to get the lay of the land."

"This is the Barkley Tableland, man," Yin said. "We've got flat for miles. We're lucky to have that little nothing town as a rest stop ahead, because aside from Darwin and Alice Springs, there's nothing."

"You've never spent much time in the wild, have you?" Bolan asked. "I can see at least five places where we can stash this SUV so that no one will even notice it."

"So let's pull off," Yin said.

Bolan shook his head. "We've got one set of eyes on us with a radio. There's also a backup, because these guys aren't amateurs. We put down one stalker, the other calls back and let's them know the game is up, so the rest of the team drops down like a hammer. This SUV's tough, but remember that artillery barrage?"

Yin nodded. "Okay."

"We stop in that little town, and I'll set something up. They won't make their move in a civilian locale."

"So we'd have a reprieve?" Yin asked.

Bolan glanced at the side mirror. "Let's say they've got a ten-mile relay behind us. We'll have a few minutes of relative peace and quiet. They'll see if they can take me out quietly, maybe a suppressed SMG at a few feet, and then they light out and disappear."

"What about me?" Yin wondered aloud.

"If you're too close, they'll take you. But they leave small fish. This way they keep the fear alive. Keeping the sheep nervous," Bolan explained. "'Course, if you act like a threat…"

Bolan leveled a finger at Yin and dropped his thumb, making a popping sound.

Yin winced. "Your plan would make me a threat?"

"What use would you be if I hung a sign making you out to be useful?" Bolan asked. "No, I'll make certain they ignore you."

"How? You got some magical cloak that makes me invisible?" Yin quizzed.

"No, Yin. I've got something better. Her."

Wangara had awakened, as if sensing the tension in the SUV. She shifted, worried.

"Huh?" Yin asked.

"She's your date for lunch. Chinese guy and an Abo girl, sitting at a diner after rolling up in these wheels?" Bolan asked. "Tourists. Leave your gun behind. They see that you're packing, you're dead."

Yin glanced into the backseat. "And how do I keep control of her?"

Bolan locked eyes with Wangara. "She won't misbehave. Right?"

The young woman nodded nervously.

"She knows if she screws this up, the dingoes will be gnawing on her bones," Bolan added. "Then again, if you screw this up, we'll all be the same brand of carrion."

Yin swallowed hard. "No worries," he said, giving Bolan a nervous grin.

"Good. Give me your pistol," Bolan said.

Yin pulled it from his waistband. The Executioner stashed it under the seat after stripping it of its magazine and the round in the chamber. His war bag, with its magazines and ammunition, was locked away in a compartment under the floorboards behind Wangara's seat.

"You're not even going to use it?" Yin asked.

"If my plan goes right, I won't need anything more than I'm wearing," Bolan told him. He rapped the door where the MP-5 was hidden. "If it screws up, the chopper in here would be useless anyway. Welcome to the big leagues, kid."

Yin's lips tightened into a bloodless line. "So…"

"The story is that you two picked up a hitchhiker. Me. I'm paying for gas down to Alice Springs. You two met in Darwin, and you're on vacation together. Young lovers," Bolan explained. "You, in the front seat. We're switching places," Bolan ordered.

Wangara crawled over the top of the seat, and Bolan slid between the passenger and driver's seat. The transition was smooth, not disturbing Yin as he drove. Wangara looked back to Bolan as he settled in.

"Think you can follow that, girl?" Bolan inquired.

She nodded. She was too scared to share a conspiratorial wink. She'd heard multiple stories so far from the big American. While he'd sounded completely honest with her earlier at the gas station, there was also the strength of truth as the assassin informed Yin of the coming conflict. She knew that Bolan was lying to Yin, leading him on with an explanation that would point the triad gangster away from the truth that he was a crusading covert crime fighter who was interested in stopping Yin's bosses. However, the man's silver tongue made everything he said seem genuine and honest. Wangara reminded herself there was no way that he could have survived as long as he had without being able to fool his enemies.

"What else?" Yin asked. "There has to be more to your plan than just me making goo-goo eyes at her and nibbling on a sandwich."

Bolan shook his head. "I'll meet up with you when everything is done. If they come for you, just stay where you are."

"As bait?" Yin asked.

"A distraction. They'll leave someone to keep an eye on you, but they won't do anything more if they notice that you're unarmed," Bolan explained. "They might try to make you into bait, but they won't pull something like a hostage situation. It'd draw too much heat, especially if there is any form of law in the area."

Bolan nodded to Wangara. "So no panic. No running away. Got it?"

"Got it," she answered.

Bolan sat back, running over his battle plan behind closed eyes.

LUCENZO AND TALARICO COASTED past the town of White-rock as their target pulled off the road and drove into a small diner parking lot. To call the minuscule collection of buildings a town was, to Lucenzo, a gross exaggeration.

"Seriously, boss, you can count the number of branches on the family tree in this place by the number of eyebrows on Talarico's face," Lucenzo quipped over the radio.

"Fuck off, asshole," Talarico snarled, eliciting a laugh from Lucenzo.

"Leave him alone," Garrett Victor ordered. "Continue on a click and then take to ground. I want long-range reconnaissance on this guy."

"We could just—"

"Can you swim from Australia to South America?" Victor asked.

"Uh, no," Lucenzo replied. "Why?"

"Because, asshole, that'd be the only safe way for you to get out of my reach. Do. As. I. Say," Victor growled into the radio. "Don't make me regret hiring your dumb wop ass. Sorry, Rico."

"No problem," Talarico replied. "This fuckin' dago gives the whole planet a bad name."

"Listen, Garrett—"

"My friends call me Garrett," Victor responded. "You, on the other hand, don't say shit to me except the intel I ask for and sir, yes, sir! Understand?"

"Sir, yes, sir," Lucenzo responded, eliciting a chuckle from Talarico.

He drove past the town, finding a sand dune to hide behind. He and Talarico parked their motorcycles, and the mercenary grumbled as he pulled a pair of binoculars from his gear bag. He crawled to the top of the eight-foot hillock. Talarico nestled beside him.

"Don't worry about Victor," Talarico said. "He treats everyone like shit, even the people he's worked with for—"

"Screw him," Lucenzo interjected. "He thinks he's hot shit because he used to be Force Recon? Everyone knows only assholes and losers join the Marines, and you only get on Force Recon by kissing ass."

Talarico's neck burned. He'd been in the Marine Corps before being dishonorably discharged. A remark like that was more than enough justification for him to take Lucenzo's head and use it for a pottery project. The only thing stopping him was that he didn't want to have to sit next to a corpse baking in the sun for the better part of an afternoon. He also guessed that Victor would want first crack at turning Lucenzo's head into an ashtray.

"Oh, that's right, you were one of Uncle Sam's Misconceived Cretins yourself, Unabrow," Lucenzo added.

"Do your fucking job, asshole," Talarico said, trying to blow off his anger and hostility.

Lucenzo grinned.

Talarico's knuckles turned white as he squeezed the rubberized body of his own set of binoculars, imagining Lucenzo's eyes popping from their sockets as his face purpled. "I'm going to get a better angle on the town," he grumbled.

"Looks like the kid and the girl went into a diner," Lucenzo spoke up. "Like it's date night."

Talarico lifted the glasses to his face. He scanned the diner, noting that Lucenzo was right. He swept the glasses around, looking for their target, the big man. It took a few moments before he spotted him, leaving a gas station. The man leaned against a wall, sipping beer from a tallboy can.

Talarico licked his lips, envious of the cold brew his target was enjoying.

"Subject sighted. He's sucking back a cold one and packing heat," Lucenzo said over the radio.

NO POSTAGE
NECESSARY
IF MAILED
IN THE
UNITED STATES

BUSINESS REPLY MAIL
FIRST-CLASS MAIL   PERMIT NO. 717   BUFFALO, NY

POSTAGE WILL BE PAID BY ADDRESSEE

GOLD EAGLE READER SERVICE
3010 WALDEN AVE
PO BOX 1867
BUFFALO NY 14240-9952

Get FREE BOOKS and a FREE GIFT when you play the...

LAS VEGAS

GAME

Just scratch off the gold box with a coin. Then check below to see the gifts you get!

YES! I have scratched off the gold box. Please send me my **2 FREE BOOKS** and **gift for which I qualify.** I understand that I am under no obligation to purchase any books as explained on the back of this card.

▼ DETACH AND MAIL CARD TODAY! ▼

366 ADL ENWS

166 ADL ENX4
(GE-LV-08)

FIRST NAME	LAST NAME

ADDRESS

APT.#	CITY

STATE/PROV.	ZIP/POSTAL CODE

7	7	7	Worth TWO FREE BOOKS plus a BONUS Mystery Gift!
🍒	🍒	🍒	Worth TWO FREE BOOKS!
🔔	🔔	♣	TRY AGAIN!

Offer limited to one per household and not valid to current subscribers of Gold Eagle® books. All orders subject to approval. Please allow 4 to 6 weeks for delivery.

Talarico glanced over to the crude loudmouth, who simply smirked back.

"Rico, pop your tire and walk it back to the town. See if you can get it patched at the station. If you can't, use the cell phone," Victor ordered. "Lucenzo, hang back and watch things."

"Sir, yes, sir," Lucenzo answered, wrinkling his nose.

"Just close and observe?" Talarico asked.

"Affirmative. No hard contact. Put your piece someplace out of sight, so you're not packing, unless you have a backup."

"Knife on my calf, and a .38 on my opposite ankle," Talarico responded, doffing his jacket to wriggle out of the shoulder holster for his pistol.

"Good thinking," Victor complimented him. "Remember, no hard contact. Eyes only."

Talarico put his jacket back on, then drove his motorcycle hard, throwing it onto a skid, his leather biker armor taking a horrendous scuffing before he used his knife to pop the tire. The armor protected him from injury, stiffened polycarbonate plates shielding his bones and joints, the leather cushioning his skin. He walked the bike back toward Whiterock, having made the accident look real.

YIN STUDIED WANGARA'S FACE as she looked at the dull plastic of the diner table in front of her.

"So what are you going to eat?" Yin asked.

"I dunno," she said, mumbling. "What about you?"

"Something quick. A sandwich or something," Yin said with a shrug. "Some chips on the side."

"Sounds good," the young woman mumbled.

Yin sighed and rolled his eyes. "Do you have to be so cheerful? People might think you're high or something."

Wangara looked up, meeting Yin's eyes. "Got a reason for me to calm down?"

The waitress came by. They ordered steak sandwiches, fries and a couple of cold beers.

"Really, you've got a reason for me to feel good?" Wangara asked.

"Well, if you talk, everything's going to come out better," Yin said. "I personally wouldn't want to hurt you. And Stone, he's looking out for you."

"What makes me so special that I'm not supposed to be afraid of a hardened triad street soldier?" she asked.

"Hardened? I'm an errand boy who grew up in Australia. You probably have more killing experience than I do," Yin said.

"Do wild hogs count?" Wangara asked.

Yin chuckled. "Anything that takes more than a shoe sole does. The biggest thing I've ever killed were some cockroaches in my Chinatown apartment."

Wangara nodded. "Okay, you got me. The biggest hog I shot only weighed three hundred pounds."

Yin covered his mouth to contain a guffaw. "The roaches in my apartment aren't that small."

Wangara broke into a smile, which weakened, melting under the reality of the situation. "We've got worse things to worry about," she said.

Yin reached out. "Listen, you don't have to worry. I'm watching out for you. Don't forget we're supposed to be on a date right now."

"You don't even have a pistol on you now," she said. She stared at his offered hand, unsure.

"Stone will give me my gun back," Yin replied. "And he's the one who said we should take care of you, not rough you up. I don't even think he wants to smack you around for answers."

"No. But he's no saint. Look at what happened at Law's," Wangara reminded him.

Yin shrugged. "Law tried to get up in his business and got all of us shot at. I don't blame Stone for walking all over that guy."

Wangara finally put her hand in his. "Sure this sudden stroke of nobility isn't something else?"

"I'd be lying if I didn't admit that you're pretty damn cute," Yin said. He gave her hand a squeeze. "Just wish I wasn't in the role of keeping you prisoner."

Wangara looked out the diner window, wondering what her grandfather would think about her if she admitted that she had fallen for the fiery young crook who started showing off a heart of gold. She looked back to Yin. "Maybe if we make it through this, we can start from scratch."

"You think?" Yin asked. "You won't hold your captivity against me?"

They paused as the waitress dropped off their plates. Wangara regarded him with a sly grin. "I've been known to be very forgiving."

Yin nodded and dug into his sandwich.

IT TOOK TEN MINUTES to reach the gas station, and by the time he got there, Talarico's shoulders were sore from steering the bike. He nodded to the Executioner and brought the bike to a halt, resting it on its kickstand.

"Ouch," Bolan said sympathetically.

"Thankfully, not too much ouch," Talarico replied honestly. "Luckily it wasn't a long walk. They have any more beer in there?"

"A full cooler," Bolan answered. "Popped your tire. I don't think they have too many bikes in town. I didn't see any tires inside."

"They have hole patch kits?" Talarico asked, removing his helmet and hanging it off the handlebar.

"Probably. I'm just passing through," Bolan said with a shrug. He took another pull of his beer. "Good luck."

"Hell, at least I beefed close enough to a cold beer," Talarico answered with a chuckle. He went inside. Bolan set down his beer and followed the mercenary through the door.

"What—" Talarico began to speak when Bolan arced a fist into the ex-Marine's kidney. The blow laced the mercenary's side with liquid flame, dropping him to his knees. Talarico tried to speak up when he felt the muzzle of Bolan's Walther pressed into the soft tissues under his jaw.

"Relax," Bolan ordered. "Using two fingers only, give me your .38 and the knife you have hidden."

"How?"

"If I could track down Wade Augustyn, I can see an amateur like you packing heat on his legs," Bolan snarled.

The gas station owner watched the drama going down. "Why, it certainly does look like he tried to rob me," the man said.

"I'd keep that shotgun handy," Bolan answered. The quick exchange convinced Talarico that Bolan had found an instant confederate in the local man behind the counter. "This punk's friends will be by, and there will be conflict."

The grizzled old Australian nodded numbly, turning his attention back to the magazine spread out on his counter. "I'd listen to that man, son. He knew I had a shotgun, and he didn't even see behind my counter. He's either psychic, or he's shot more people than you've seen in your life-time."

Talarico tossed his gun and his gravity knife onto the tiled floor by the counter. "How do you know he isn't going to hurt you?" he asked.

The old man looked at Talarico, then sighed. "Look at this dive. The only thing worth stealing is the beer, and he paid for that. What's he gonna shoot me for?"

"Welcome to the outback," Bolan said, dragging Talarico toward the restroom. Using a pair of cable ties, he bound the man to the sink. It took only a few moments for Bolan to find Talarico's hands-free radio and pull it off him. He inserted the earpiece and tucked the rest of the unit into his pocket, leaving the mercenary in the dark behind a closed door.

"Head to the back office," Bolan suggested to the store owner.

The old man started there, then unplugged the mini-fridge full of beer and rolled it in the back after tossing his double-barreled shotgun atop it. "Can't afford to lose this. That boy's friends come in here shooting, I'll need something solid to hide behind."

Bolan nodded. "I'll keep most of the drama out of the

way. Can I borrow that old pickup you've got around the back?"

The old man thought for a moment. "What the hell, it's not much use to me. 'Sides, it's not like bullet holes would take away from the rust holes, right?"

Bolan shook his head.

"What started all of this, if you don't mind?" the old man asked.

"I thought I'd have a simple job taking out a bad guy in Hong Kong," Bolan explained.

The old man nodded sagely. "Life never turns out like you expect it, eh?"

"Nope," Bolan answered. "But I try to plan ahead."

"Good luck, son," the gas station owner replied, tossing him a pair of keys. Bolan snatched them out of the air and headed outside.

9

The Executioner wandered in front of the diner and flashed Yin a hand signal that they'd agreed upon.

Yin paid for his and Wangara's meals, and together, the trio got into the big BMW SUV. Bolan, however, didn't settle into the backseat but stole out of the far door. Yin peeled out, kicking up a large enough dust cloud to conceal the Executioner as he rushed toward the pickup truck.

Lucenzo's voice was loud over Bolan's confiscated hands-free radio, sputtering in continued panic over the sudden abduction of Talarico.

"They're bugging out! They're heading my way!" Lucenzo announced.

"Keep a low profile and track 'em," came the response from the other end. "Avoid hard contact. You've flushed them, and you don't have the firepower to take down that ride!"

"Sir, yes, sir," Lucenzo replied, sounding less than convincing as an obedient soldier.

Bolan slid behind the wheel of the old Ford pickup. It had seen a better century, and the store owner hadn't been kidding about the gaping holes eaten by rust over the years. Still, when he fired up the engine, it turned over at once, throbbing with power and confidence. Bolan eased the truck out of position, fully aware that Lucenzo was occupied. He could hear the rustling sounds of leather on his throat mike as the mercenary suited back up and climbed onto his motorcycle. The Executioner tore off up the road, racing to a spot he'd picked out on the approach into town, one of the spots he'd told Yin he could hide an SUV. Backing in, he was glad to see the dust settle from his dash to cover. He took out his Desert Eagle, checked it for dust, operating the thumb safety to be certain of it. With a stroke of his thumb, it was ready to launch a 240-grain slug with a caress of its 4.5 pound trigger. Still, as powerful as the .44 Magnum round was, Bolan doubted that it would do much more than cause a minor blemish on the shell of whatever vehicle the mercenaries were using, so he stuffed it back in its holster. Indeed, none of Bolan's arsenal could do much against armor plating.

Instead of relying on his limited firepower, Bolan kept the engine idling. He had a ton of weaponry rumbling, waiting for a press of the gas pedal to launch it. All he had to do was wait, and having convinced the mercenary death squad that he'd been flushed, the killers were misdirected into racing at full speed to catch up with the BMW. Sure enough, a Land Rover raced by, and Bolan stomped the gas, the Ford lurching out. Building up speed to overtake the Land Rover was easy with the old truck's reserves of power. He moved the pickup into the Land Rover's blind spot long enough to accelerate faster.

Too late, one of the men in the back of the mercenary's

SUV noticed the rust bucket lancing toward them like a missile. Bolan aimed for the rear tire, and his fender connected with the Land Rover's rear axle in a classic pit maneuver. When the Ford hit the SUV in its rear wheel, the precision impact shattered their drive train. Steel snapped due to unexpected stresses, and the vehicle spun like a top, careening off the road. It hit a rut in the sand and exploded into a tumble, throwing up clouds of sand as it rolled wildly out of control.

Bolan skidded the pickup to a halt, jumping out the driver's side door. He had the Desert Eagle up in a two-handed grip, safety swiped off with a stroke of his thumb. Since it had taken Bolan a few moments to bring his pickup to a halt, he'd lost the brief window where all the mercenaries in the truck would be rendered completely stunned. The SUV had been upended, its front wheels still whirling as the engine revved in idle, the right rear tire that Bolan had smashed in the pit maneuver hanging by a thread of mangled axle.

The driver's side doors were pinned to the dirt, but the passenger door kicked open, the slam of a boot on it accompanied by an enraged grunt. The Executioner circled around the vehicle, keeping his eye on the opened door as a body flopped to the ground, scurrying to get out of the crashed vehicle. Blood gushed from a five-inch gash across the man's forehead, making his face a crimson mask. Bolan was about to pass on the mercenary, assuming him to be too incapacitated to provide a threat when he saw the gleam of a pistol slide poking from his hand.

"Bastard!" the would-be ambusher snarled.

Bolan answered the curse with a single .44 Magnum

slug that speared through the bridge of the blood-splat-
tered nose. The mercenary jerked violently, his silver
handgun chugging a round into the dirt at his feet in dying
reflex.

More cries of dismay erupted from the vehicle as the
upside-down driver was showered with gore and the deformed .44 Magnum slug clipped across his abdominal
muscles. He shrieked. "I'm hit! He shot me! He shot me!"

The mercenaries might have been professional soldiers,
but composure accounted only for so much. Smashed off
the road and turned upside down, then covered with brains,
the driver's nerves had broken like brittle glass.

Heavy safety glass bubbled and deformed as a panicked gunner in the rear opened fire with his weapon. The
initial burst hadn't been sufficient to do more than pro-
duce a three-inch stretch and bulge in the armored safety
glass, but the Executioner wasn't going to stand still for
long. A second burst followed the first, the M-4 carbine
stitching through the window frame. Bolan had sidestepped in time to avoid a sizzling burst of autofire. He
tripped the Desert Eagle's trigger twice, hammering out
big Magnum rounds toward the rifleman.

The M-4 chattered again, ripping out more high-velocity hornets that came dangerously close to stitching Bolan,
a shoulder roll having protected him from death. The gunner in the back had clearly been wearing armor, enough
to protect him from a .44 Magnum slug. The Executioner
respected the man's preparations, and knew that the dead
gunner had been a new hire. The man Bolan knew only
as Garrett and his core team would most likely have been
wearing heavy-duty Kevlar armor, but had neglected to

provide it to their recent pawns. Tucked deep in the cabin of the Land Rover, Garrett was out of Bolan's line of sight, making an aimed shot difficult, especially since exposure long enough to make target acquisition would leave him vulnerable to a follow-up blast of M-4 fire.

Bolan retreated toward the pickup truck, moving in a serpentine fashion, whirling out of the path of rifle bullets as the mercenary tried to track him. Bolan dived behind the fender of the ancient Ford, listening to the rattle of 5.56 mm rounds clanking against the fender. The Executioner dumped his partially spent magazine and topped it off with a fresh one, letting the enemy rifleman burn up time and ammunition. With a glance around the frame of the truck, Bolan saw the rear door of the Land Rover swing open. One of Garrett's men exited the vehicle with a compact rifle in his fists. The man and the Executioner saw each other at the same time, both of them opening fire in the same instant.

The dazed and stunned mercenary hadn't had time to shoulder his weapon and get a proper sight picture. Bullets chewed the dirt to one side of Bolan. The Executioner's Desert Eagle, however, was lined up on the would-be assassin's face. A .44 Magnum round crashed through the man's eye socket.

In the Land Rover, Garrett Victor saw Evans, his fellow former Marine, collapse in a heap as his head ejected gore. With Evans and Esar both down, he only had Stoffer and their driver, Cage, who was busy in the middle of an all-out panic.

"He's got us pinned," Stoffer exclaimed.

"He's only got a handgun," Victor responded.

"He shot me in the fucking stomach!" Cage yowled.

Victor punched the panicked driver in the back of the head. "He only nicked you. If you'd been smart enough to wear that armor I gave you—"

The door panel smashed to splinters as another .44 Magnum round slammed into it, missing Victor by inches. The ex-Marine milked the M-4's trigger, hosing out an arc of fire.

"We need to coordinate, damn it," Victor snarled. "Stoff—"

Stoffer had lunged and grabbed Evans's rifle, pulling it to him. "Grenade," he shouted.

"Now we're thinking," Victor said. He jammed a machine pistol into Cage's hands. "Open fire, dumb shit—"

"He'll kill me," Cage whimpered. "I'm just—"

Victor fired through the back of the seat, Cage's chest erupting with spurts of gore, spraying the windshield with his blood. "Goddamned amateur hour. Stoff, pump some high explosives into that shit! I'll cover you."

Victor slid prone and ripped out a series of short bursts, slicing his rounds under the chassis of the pickup truck, keeping Bolan pinned down. The Executioner used the protection of the Ford's wheels for his feet, but the protection also served as a prison for him. Stoffer lanced a 40 mm blooper into the pickup's cab.

Bolan heard the all too familiar thump of an M-203 grenade launcher and threw himself in a dive toward a roadside ditch, arms spread to catch enough air to help him sail a few more feet. He landed, folding into a ball, and rolled to the bottom of the ditch in time to avoid the slashing sheet of shrapnel that 6.5 ounces of high explosives turned the rusted-out Ford into. The pickup snapped in two, vomiting up a blossom of fire. The concussive wave rolled over Bolan, and he could feel it like a rolling pin, compressing his skin and muscle against his bones. Then the instant pressure was gone, but it left Bolan dazed.

Rifle fire lanced at the wreckage of the rusted-out Ford, then swept away from the burning hulk. Divots of dirt spewed into the sky as Victor and Stoffer raked the area. Bolan, flattened to the bottom of the roadside runoff, was out of their field of fire, but he knew that wouldn't last long as the duo advanced slowly. The mercenaries had been taken off guard by the Executioner once, and they weren't going to make any more mistakes.

From the angles of dirt puffs, Bolan could tell that the pair had spread out, forming a perpendicular cross fire. At a ninety-degree angle, they were safe from hitting each other, but they could maximize their coverage. When one stopped to reload, the other continued laying down a flaming spear of bullets.

The two suddenly held up, the rattle of rifles fallen silent. They had scanned the pickup and learned that Bolan had escaped the grenade blast. Since the ditch was the only cover he could have reached, Victor and Stoffer were leery of pressing their advance any further. They'd lost Talarico, Evans and Esar to their underestimation. They'd learned their lesson the hardest way, and they weren't going to spend the lives of their partners lightly.

On his belly, Bolan was able to crawl twenty feet through the ditch, staying out of the sight of the mercenaries, senses alert for the eventuality that they'd noticed his movements.

Stoffer triggered the M-203 again, planting a bomb into the ditch. The HE shell went up, spraying a cloud of dust. Protected by the uneven floor of the ditch, Bolan had avoided the lethal radius of the grenade's blast. The overpressure wave rocked him, his ears ringing from the force that slammed into him.

"No movement," Victor's voice came over the radio. The earbud that Bolan wore hadn't been knocked loose, but then the LASH unit was designed for use in combat. The mercenary leader kept his voice low, but over the radio, it was crystal clear, especially since the earbud had protected Bolan's hearing in that ear. Bolan was torn between removing the bud so he could hear the two mercenaries, or continuing to listen to their radio communications. Bolan compromised, slipping the earbud to his off ear.

The pair wasn't charging in. They were hoping the Executioner would reveal himself. It was a waiting game, and with two pairs of eyes, they had an advantage. Two men could cover gaps in the other's perception and watch out for their partner. If Bolan could take down one, the other would still be in a position to take him down. He slid the Desert Eagle back into its holster, drawing the suppressed Walther P-99. He needed to make the most of the element of surprise, and even though the sound-suppressed 9 mm round still would make a noise, he could use every little bit of help he could get.

One man stepped into view, but his gaze passed over the Executioner who had been caked with settling dust from the grenade blasts and fusillades of automatic fire that had chopped the dirt into free flying clouds. Bolan had brushed loose soil over the Walther, preventing it from glinting in the sun. He lined up the end of his suppressor up with the man, and pulled the trigger just a hair breadth too late, the 9 mm pill popping softly through the air and grazing the merc's shoulder rather than coring him through the face. The glancing gunshot elicited a grunt of fear from the second man, who cut loose with a burst of autofire, raking the ground two feet from the Executioner's right side.

Bolan took the opportunity to fire, aiming low. His Walther punched two holes in the mercenary's leg. The 9 mm impacts knocked the limb out from under him, his rifle clattering to the bottom of the roadside ditch as he crashed to his face.

"Stoff!" Victor growled. The ex-Marine's rifle hammered on full-auto, and Bolan lunged away from his hiding spot only moments before the first salvo of bullets speared into the ground. The Executioner returned fire, 9 mm rounds rocking into Victor's center of mass. While the Kevlar armor managed to hold, reflex and instinct sent the mercenary diving for cover. Bolan launched forward, diving at the merc. More than two hundred pounds plowed through Victor's midsection. While the 9 mm bullets didn't possess the momentum to move a human being, the Executioner's mass picked the gunman up off all fours and speared him against the smoldering wreckage of the Ford pickup.

The mercenary reached for the knife he had in a hip sheath, but Bolan interrupted the draw by crashing the steel-magazine reinforced polymer and fiberglass frame of the Walther across his forearm with bone-breaking force. With the snap of his ulna, Victor lost the ability to maintain a grip. Bolan lashed the crown of his head across Victor's jaw, creating an explosion of nerve misfires that rocked the ex-Marine harder than both 40 mm grenades had shaken Bolan.

Victor flopped to the dirt, and Bolan snapped a hard fist into the base of the gunman's neck. The blow staked the would-be assassin to the ground, not to get up for a long time.

Stoffer, one hand clamped over his ravaged leg, fumbled for the pistol in his hip holster. Bolan hauled Victor up as a shield just as the wounded mercenary's sidearm cracked, bullets snapping through the air and being stopped cold by Kevlar body armor. With a lurch, the Executioner smashed Victor's body against the hobbled assassin, bodies sandwiched onto the road. Stoffer's ribs cracked under Bolan and Victor's combined weight, taking the fight out of him.

Bolan checked Stoffer's leg. The blood seeped from his torn thigh, instead of jetting out with arterial force. He knew that it would only take a quick pressure bandage to keep him from bleeding to death. The cold-blooded execution of unarmed, helpless prisoners was never part of Bolan's plan. He rolled Victor onto his back, checking for a pulse and respiration.

Now he had three live prisoners instead of one.

Stoffer coughed, wincing as the convulsion aggravated his broken ribs. "Hurts…bad."

"No kidding," Bolan replied. "Eugene Waylon hired some good people, but I'm still here."

"Good trap," Stoffer wheezed. "Why not pull the trigger if you know that Waylon sent us?"

Bolan shook his head. "You're alive because you're not a threat anymore. I disarmed you, broke you and rendered you harmless. I don't need to kill you. As for your friend, I don't kill unconscious foes."

Bolan took out his cell phone and took photos of both men for further identification. He hit transmit to send the digital images back to Stony Man Farm. "You'll live, and you'll carry the message. Waylon picked the wrong man to back in Wade Augustyn."

Stoffer nodded, pain racking his face.

"Limp to your car and call your friend driving around Darwin," Bolan said in a show of omniscence that sent a visible chill through Stoffer. "Have him pick you and this lump of meat up, and then you run very far away."

"He'll want a piece of you," Stoffer said.

Bolan looked down at Victor, then stepped on his fractured forearm. The crack of the arm bones sounded like gunshots. "Have him call me when he has two hands to hold a gun. Until then, let him know how lucky he was to survive this day."

The Executioner turned and walked toward his rendezvous with Yin and Wangara.

10

Bobby Yeung bristled when the phone call came in.

"Boss, this cat you hired is the real shit," Yin said.

"Why?" Yeung asked.

Yin's answer chilled the triad boss to the bone. "The Americans are after him. An American death squad came after him."

Yeung lowered the phone from his ear, sucking in two deep breaths, trying to recover his nerves. After ten seconds of listening to Yin calling out, he brought the phone back to his face. "Can you be sure?"

"I just listened to what sounded like World War III, boss. Grenades and automatic rifles ripping the place apart. He told me to split off with him, said he had a plan, and then the next thing I know, it looks like someone decided to bomb the desert just north of this town we'd stopped in," Yin explained. "I saw a pickup truck go up."

"What did he tell you to do?" Yeung inquired.

"Told me to make it look like we were leaving town," Yin responded. "He got in the back, but ducked out as I kicked up dust to leave. He must have taken the pickup to interrupt—"

Yeung tensed, the other side of the phone going almost silent, inarticulate murmurs in two different voices. The next thing he heard was the Executioner's voice.

"Don't worry. The Americans are done. I took care of them."

"Stone?" Yeung was stunned. "But…Yin told me your truck blew up."

"Yeah. Would have been impressive if I wasn't outside of it," Bolan replied. "It took some doing, but I finally resolved the issue. I'm not adding this to your tab. I'm the one who pissed them off."

"Damn it, Stone—"

"I said don't worry. I'm alive. I'm continuing on. Nobody in town knows anything about what happened. They just heard gunfire," Bolan explained. "Unless you found Grandfather Wangara…"

"Not on an open line," Yeung said.

"You were already talking about the Americans," Bolan said. "You've probably been flagged and listened to for several minutes. So, to any Feds listening on the line, find yourself another death squad. I broke yours."

Yeung's lower spine spasmed in an explosion of twitches, realizing that he'd called down the lightning to the facility. First came Wangara's inspiration to the Aboriginal leaders to rebel against the invasion of their sacred lands, then Law's sudden rebellion and now the attack of an American death squad. Yeung was suddenly homesick for Hong Kong, where he knew the players who wanted a piece of him. Out in the middle of nowhere in Australia, he was exposed and vulnerable. "Stone!"

"I'm still on my way. Don't worry, Bobby," Bolan said.

The phone line went dead. Yeung staggered to his feet and lurched toward the bathroom. He didn't even have the time to reach a toilet. He bent over a sink and released the contents of his stomach in an explosion of terror-induced nausea. He turned on the faucet and splashed water on his face, rinsing the bile off his chin while his back and shoulders trembled. He fought against himself, willing his body to stop reacting to the fears rocketing through his mind, but his knees turned to rubber and he nearly barked his jaw on the edge of the sink. He collapsed to all fours.

What had been under his iron control only until a day ago was spiraling into mayhem. The facility was supposed to be a covert operation, drawing little or no attention, and in the past few days, the city of Darwin had exploded in two major gunfights. Violence wasn't common in northern Australia, the Black Rose soldiers carrying weapons as badges of honor, symbols of their toughness rather than an actual need to deal with other gangsters from a position of power. To have nearly thirty Chinese gunmen end up dead in the space of twenty-four hours would put the Australian government on alert.

Yeung's pockets had been made deep for operating the facility primarily for the purpose of paying off officials to look the other way on minor criminal activities that were the smoke screen for the true plan. However, the bodies piled up in the morgue was something that Yeung didn't think he could make go away by throwing money at it.

Yeung smashed the edge of his fist against the tiled bathroom floor, using the sudden pain jolting from wrist to pinky knuckle to focus. He latched on to the sudden ache, feeding on it, drawing strength and will from it. He rose, still shaky, to his feet, and looked at himself in the mirror. His dark eyes burned angrily, challenging him to be harder than the weakling who dropped to his knees. He brushed aside his sun-lightened hair, now the color of burnished brass, settling down poking spikes rising up from the back of his head. He gulped down deep breaths.

"Stone took care of Law and the Americans," he told his reflection. "I'm still in charge. I haven't received the call from the top telling me that I'm dead."

He curled back his lips, revealing the grin of an iron-hard warrior, his hand dropping to the Walther stuffed into his waistband. "You're Bobby Yeung. Black Rose Triad. You are a god compared to everyone around you."

Yeung straightened his collar and took a paper towel to dry the moisture from his face, tossing it into the wastebasket with a perfect throw, hitting the center in a swish. The fear rocketed away, and he smirked to his reflection.

"Bobby Yeung, represent."

He slammed open the bathroom door and strode into the lobby.

LUCENZO SKIDDED his motorcycle to a halt, kicking up a cloud of dust that hung in the air, obscuring Garrett Victor and Julius Stoffer as they walked slowly toward Whiterock. Victor's arm was folded across his chest, bound in place by a belt. The mercenary leader's face was pale and damp, the pain of a shattered limb reducing his hard, rugged features to a clammy mask trying to hold back a flood of suffering. Stoffer limped, his leg wrapped, sleeves torn from his shirt in an improvised bandage. He leaned on Victor for support.

Neither man retained their firearms.

"Do you mind?" Stoffer grimaced, waving road dust away from his face.

"What the fuck happened?" Lucenzo cursed. "Where are the others?"

"We're it," Victor rasped. "We're the only survivors."

Lucenzo's eyes narrowed. He saw that Victor's forearm was wrapped, the front of his shirt drenched with blood. "What?"

"Piece of bone broke the skin," Victor said, his voice rough as broken gravel. "Took a while to control the bleeding. I'd have died without Stoff. As it is, my job's over."

"Over?" Lucenzo asked. "He's still—"

"My whole fucking career is over, you stupid little shit," Victor snarled. "We had to pull an inch of bone out through my skin. My damned shooting hand is worthless."

"You're going to let him get away with that?" Lucenzo snapped.

"I'm alive. It means I can probably get some kind of work. You want this bastard, take your shot," Victor told him. "He owned me once, and I had four men with automatic weapons on my side while all he had was a handgun and a rusty old pickup. I'm not going after him again, not even with an army."

"Coward," Lucenzo murmured.

"A realist, damn it," Stoffer said. "Who do you have left? Talarico? If he's even alive…"

Lucenzo took a deep breath. "Where's the rest of the guns?"

"Well, if you hadn't hot dogged over here, you could see the trickle of smoke rising from where we crashed. They're in the SUV," Victor answered. "You're welcome to 'em. It's your funeral."

Lucenzo pulled his Beretta from under his jacket, aiming at the ex-Marine. "Fuck off."

Garrett Victor looked down the barrel of the 9 mm pistol, unflinching.

Lucenzo lowered the hammer on his Beretta and stuck it back under his jacket. "You're pathetic, Garrett. It's worse to let a punk like you live."

Victor jerked his head to one side. "Go get your gun, Johnny. If you make it through this alive, look me up and maybe I'll think you're worth a shit."

Lucenzo revved the engine, releasing the rear brake enough to kick up a thick new choking cloud of dust, forcing Victor and Stoffer into fits of coughing, before racing off.

Left as human wreckage, Victor still wasn't impressed by him. Lucenzo knew the only way to regain his manhood was to take on their target and take him down. He was scared. Anyone who could leave a Marine team dead and crippled was indeed a tough guy.

Alone, he was going to have to take down a one-man army who had seen him coming once before, and was sharp enough to take down a savvy crew of special-operations-capable veterans. His stomach turned, but he knew that if he could get a good rifle from the cracked-up SUV, he'd have the mystery assassin at his mercy. He was going to come down like a hammer, striking from surprise.

Maybe it would be enough.

THE BMW ROLLED INTO Alice Springs, abandoning the desolation of the lonely road for a tourist mecca that sprawled out. The official population was only 26,000, but there were easily twice that many people in the area, as its placement in the center of the continent, away from the tablelands, made it pleasant and mild. Its proximity to the great Uluru mound, the sprawling ranch lands and Aboriginal territories made it a popular tourist attraction. Because of the influx of tourism dollars, Alice Springs had grown, not so much in population, but in facilities. Bolan saw resort complexes splayed out, designed to be low profile and attractive additions to the landscape, rather than jutting upward garishly.

The crowds of tourists were evenly spread out, giving the Executioner pause as he measured the potential for a deadly cross fire where civilian noncombatants would be involved. He unhooked the holster for his Desert Eagle and slipped it into his war bag, securing it under the floorboards.

"Why are you taking off your cannon?" Yin asked.

"If I take a shot on the street, anyone I hit with it will be cored through and through," Bolan answered. "I use that hog leg as a concealable rifle, but I don't want to hit a tourist on the other side of an opponent."

"Your code," Yin said, nodding sagely. "Your 9 mm won't punch through anyone, though."

"Less likely," Bolan admitted. "But I still don't want to get into it."

"We're just meeting Big Brother Bobby," Yin said. "Unless you're going to bust a cap into him."

"No," Bolan answered. He wasn't going to burn down Yeung, not when the mysterious project still needed to be discovered and shut down completely. A gunfight in Alice Springs was far from his intention, but he thought of Frankie Law. Would Law make a move in town, or would he wait for Bolan to make good on his promise to take down the facility? Bolan scanned the crowds, looking for typical triad tough men, but not feeling reassured when he found none.

Ideally, Law would make his move at the facility, where he could deflect suspicions of his rebellion as mobilizing to defend the Black Rose's investment. Given the gear that Kurtzman had heard Law was gathering, it seemed like a strong possibility, but there was always a chance that violence could erupt anywhere. Bolan never entered an area without being constantly aware of his surroundings, the potential for innocents to be harmed, fields of fire and places that would provide cover, both to utilize them, or defeat their protective properties. The SUV pulled into a hotel parking lot, and Yin deftly maneuvered into a parking spot.

Two triad gunmen, wearing black suits with white shirts, collars open, ties a discarded thought, waited, their eyes shielded by black eyeglasses. Bolan got out and walked to them, arms out to the side.

"Bobby trusts you," one guard said, noting the hanging outline of the Walther under his armpit. The two men looked Wangara over.

"She's unarmed," Bolan said.

"Sure?" the other asked.

"Golly no," Bolan responded. "I just thought I'd threaten her with torture and not make sure she can't stick a knife in my ribs."

"We're paid to be certain," the first man told Bolan.

The Executioner nodded. "Make sure your hands are polite."

The second one developed a tic at the corner of his mouth.

Bolan looked at the disappointed bodyguard. "This isn't fun time. Find yourself a hooker if you want to cop an easy feel."

"You're treading on my nerves," the second guard told him. "That's not a healthy habit."

Yin chuckled.

"Something funny?" the guard asked.

"You know who you're talking to?" Yin returned. "This guy is so hard he makes diamond look like marshmallow."

The loudmouth lowered his sunglasses so dark eyes stared over the black lenses. "All I see is a too-tall long nose who thinks he knows my business."

Bolan took a deep breath, then interposed his palm between their faces. He stepped around the bodyguard, fully aware that he had insultingly dismissed the Chinese man. The Black Rose bodyguard snarled under his breath. The Executioner ignored him, not caring about what he had to say. He'd made an enemy, but his business was with Bobby Yeung, not his spoiled little soldiers.

The triad thug took a step toward Wangara, but Yin interposed himself. "Your friend has it. Back away."

"You know who I am?" the second guard asked. "I'm Shen Wang."

The first bodyguard didn't frisk Wangara with his bare hands, instead using a small nylon baton that he stroked along her curves, finding nothing hidden in her clothes. "She's clean," he said.

Shen snorted in derision. "For a filthy little—"

Bolan had enough and grabbed Shen by the throat, dragging him into the hotel, thumb pressed deep into an artery just behind the corner of his jaw. The pressure left the man helpless, his brain deprived of oxygen, and the pain of Bolan's fingertips stabbing into nerve clusters along his neck filling the triad man with paralyzing pain. The Executioner led Shen into the lobby. It was empty except for Bobby Yeung and three of his bodyguards. The silence was thick and palpable. One of the bodyguards stood, ready to throw himself in front of Yeung, the others' hands hovering near their handguns.

"Bobby," Bolan called out.

Yeung stood, one eyebrow raised at the sight of one of his men being manhandled like a stuffed doll. "Stone? What's wrong?"

Bolan dragged Shen around, then let go. The Black Rose hard case collapsed to his hands and knees at Yeung's feet. "This one has to learn manners."

"You fucking arrogant—" Shen began.

Yeung kicked him in the elbow, and his face crashed into the floor at Yeung's feet. "Shut up."

He smirked and nodded to Bolan. "Good help is hard to find. I humor him because he's really good at breaking knees."

"His own or other people's?" Bolan quipped.

"Usually other people's, but sometimes we have to discipline him back in line," Yeung replied.

Shen looked up, enraged, but holding his tongue as blood dripped like thick syrup over his lips and off his chin onto Yeung's shoe.

"Apologize to Mr. Stone," Yeung ordered.

Shen glanced toward Bolan, fighting back the urge to leap at the man who'd paralyzed him. "I'm very sorry, Mr. Stone."

"Apology accepted," Bolan returned. "Now let's get down to business."

Yeung rubbed the top of his bloodied shoe on Shen's jacket, then walked to join the Executioner.

11

John Lucenzo rolled through Alice Springs on the back of his motorcycle. He'd wrapped his M-4 rifle in a blanket, hooking it under the seat. A range bag loaded with magazines and spare ammunition hung off the side of the bike. He wouldn't be able to draw the rifle quickly if he spotted his target, but at least he could travel far and discretely without worrying that someone would stop him because he had an assault rifle.

Traffic wasn't too thick, and as he slowly crawled through town, he kept his eyes peeled for the black BMW SUV that his prey was traveling in. If he could find the SUV, then he'd be able to track the mysterious assassin who'd cowed Victor and Stoffer, leaving the other members of the mercenary team as a pile of corpses.

Lucenzo would have loved to have the opportunity to take down the big man in black, preferably from a hundred yards, and use a whole magazine on him. In town, however, he wouldn't have the opportunity for that. There were cops around, and interested in keeping the peace in this tourist town, they'd keep an eye out for trouble. A stocky little Mediterranean with an automatic weapon would draw attention from them like a rod attracted lightning. Alice Springs wasn't going to be the spot of his showdown with the one-man army. It would only be a point where he picked up on the enemy.

The phone in his pocket warbled, and he pulled his bike over before answering it. "Who is this?"

"Waylon," came the answer. "You're still on the case?"

"I take it you spoke with that pussy Victor," Lucenzo replied. "Yeah. I'm still in this."

"Are you crazy?" Waylon asked.

"I'm pissed, not insane," Lucenzo told him. "You going to try to talk me out of taking this guy down?"

"Far from it," Waylon answered, a sigh of relief in his voice. "You're the only one who's going to keep *me* from ending up dead."

"That bad?" Lucenzo inquired.

Waylon sighed. "I lost my meal ticket to the guy you're hunting. I need him gone, otherwise the Black Rose is going to cut off my head."

"I'm not doing this for love of Victor. I'm going to do this to show that arrogant shit who the real tough guy is," Lucenzo answered. "'Course if you're still paying…"

"You've got it all coming to you," Waylon promised. "Just live long enough to collect."

"So what's going on?" Lucenzo asked. "Where is he going?"

"The Black Rose has an operation on Aboriginal tribe lands, and they hired my guy to clean out some troublemakers. This guy killed him and took the job," Waylon explained. "He's some kind of crazy shit vigilante who's got it in his head that he can take on a triad all by himself. As far as I understand, there've been a rash of shootings in Darwin and major Chinese orgcrime players are down."

"Gunfights," Lucenzo repeated. "Not assassinations?"

"Bullets flying both ways. No losses on his side, large groups of corpses left behind." Waylon broke it down for him. "This guy is scary."

"He's a fighter, not an assassin. And from the way he blindsided Victor and the others, he's got tactical training beyond any Special Forces vet. We're talking someone who has lived a long time taking on impossible odds on a regular basis," Lucenzo replied. "This guy isn't official, because he hits and leaves bodies. He doesn't arrest survivors. He just lets everyone else pick up the pieces."

"I was thinking a black operation," Waylon suggested.

"No," Lucenzo mused. "He either has a death wish, or he just doesn't give a fuck. Either way, there's no way to spook him into the open."

Waylon cut through Lucenzo's rising mist of doubt. "You will be able to take care of this asshole, right?"

Lucenzo looked up. In the lot across the street from him, he suddenly saw his quarry. It was the same SUV, right down to the license plate he'd been studying.

"Lucenzo?" Waylon called.

"Yeah. I can take care of him," the mercenary replied. He looked around the lot. A pair of Chinese men in black suits with mirrored sunglasses watched over the lot, like vigilant gargoyles. "It's just going to take some time."

"I've got time and money. Just don't let the Black Rose learn that I've sent them the devil, not their hired killer," Waylon admonished.

Lucenzo rested his hand on the butt of his Beretta as the Hong Kong businessman hung up. A subdued murmur poured out over his lips as he felt the bulk of the big 9 mm pistol in his waistband. "So close, and yet so far…"

He got off the bike and found a diner with a view of the hotel lot. The hunt was on.

"TAKE YOUR JACKET OFF and pour yourself a drink," Yeung said as he strode into his suite and dropped in a deep, comfortable chair.

"Nice place," Bolan said, letting his leather jacket slide off his shoulders, revealing his shoulder holster and the knives taped to his forearms. Yin and Wangara stood in the foyer, not quite certain how things were going down. Bolan ignored them, draped his jacket over a hook and walked toward the wet bar.

"If you like it, I can arrange for you to have a permanent room here," Yeung said. "On me."

"Meeting my bosses even once is risking my cover as your independent asset," Bolan responded. He selected a square crystal bottle filled with Cognac and poured two fingers in the bottom of a tumbler.

"A connoisseur?" Yeung asked, nodding in approval at how Bolan canted the tumbler so the Cognac wouldn't be bruised.

Bolan held the glass to the Black Rose boss. "I've learned a few things here and there."

Yeung accepted the glass and Bolan poured himself a drink, setting the crystal decanter back on the bar. "Just so we're clear. The Americans were after you, not the Black Rose Triad, right?"

"I took care of my rent," Bolan said. "You don't operate in Hong Kong with my kind of impunity without paying your dues."

Yeung nodded. "And what warranted the Americans?"

"A CIA agent or two," Bolan answered. "One of their agents got a cell-phone photo of me before I retired her."

"What's to keep the Americans from targeting Alice Springs with a tactical nuke?" Yeung inquired.

"Well, first, I killed all of them," Bolan said. He took a sip. "Second, the American teams are supposed to hit and fade."

"You're sure you killed them all," Yeung pressed.

Bolan looked pensive, putting on a show. Of course he was aware of the second motorcyclist eluding the dead or wounded fates of the rest of his mercenary team, but he wanted to plant an idea in Yeung's head. "The Americans don't nuke people, and they don't destroy entire cities to kill one man. If there's still one loose…"

"Could there be?" Yeung asked, sitting up, his shoulders visibly tensed.

"Yin, you said you saw two guys on motorcycles?" Bolan set up the question.

"Yeah, but only one came back," Yin said. "But didn't you think they were leapfrogging?"

"But those were usually just observers," Bolan said, his brow furrowing.

"We can flip this town over if we want," Yeung offered.

"No, no good," Bolan answered. "We let him know we're looking for him, he might call in someone else. Just keep an eye open, I'll take care of things."

"Why you?" Yeung asked.

Bolan glared at the triad boss. "Shen. Frankie Law. Need I say more?"

Yeung nodded, remembering how deftly the man had manhandled the Black Rose leg breaker. "Right. You and the Americans are on a level above us."

Bolan smiled.

"What about the girl? Did you get anything out of her yet?" Yeung asked.

"I'm brokering with that," Bolan told him. "She wants a guarantee you won't come after her."

"Brokering?" Yeung asked with a chuckle. "Why the fuck should I do anything for her?"

"Because she knows exactly where Grandfather Wangara went," Bolan stated. "And without that knowledge, you've got the rest of the tribe thinking that you don't hold all the cards."

Yeung sneered. "I brought you in to shoot some people for me, Stone. Not make deals with snotty teenagers."

Bolan shrugged. "Bobby, you're trying to clear out opposing leadership. She knows where the hardest of the resistance is, and she wants to live. Is that such a tough trade? A bony girl for an old Aborigine?"

Yeung sipped his drink, swirling the liquor in his tumbler in time with the thoughts turning in his head. "Stone, I'm riding the edge here. I have an attempted coup by Frankie Law, I've got you chased by assassins, and I've got the facility's security threatened by human cockroaches. I need this situation resolved. Finished. Everyone giving me hell has to die, and not next week, not tomorrow, now. Rip the information out of her."

"Hey, it's your carpet," Bolan said, slipping out a knife.

Yeung's two silent bodyguards tensed at the sight of the gleaming blade.

"You promised!" Wangara shouted. Yin froze, eyes wide with the realization that things were going wrong. The young triad man stepped in front of the Aboriginal teen to shield her, hand hovering near the butt of his pistol.

"Stone?" Yin asked.

"I have a job to do," Bolan said. "And your boss doesn't care how I do it."

"Big Brother Bobby, please," Yin pleaded, still in front of Wangara, his fingers squeezing the rubber grip panels of his pistol. "She's willing to deal. She'll squeal, and just walk away."

"Walk away?" Yeung asked. "Come on, she'll run to the cops first thing."

Yin glared at Bolan, who winked. "The cops? You think the tribes trust the cops? How do you think we got so far without police pressure?" Yin said.

"I've greased some palms," Yeung answered.

"They didn't get their own lands back until the mid-eighties," Yin countered. "They don't give a shit about the Australian government."

"It's true," Wangara said, squeezing Yin's shoulder.

Yeung sighed. "Grandfather Wangara seems willing to go to the cops."

"That's the old man!" Wangara exclaimed. "He thinks there's some magic in the dirt."

"Not you?" Yeung inquired.

The young woman thought about her grandfather's prediction, about Stone's arrival, and how he'd protected her. So far, he'd turned one enemy into a staunch defender, willing to put himself between a trained killer and her. That kind of protection was only a sliver of the true shielding the big warrior had provided for her, but it was a brilliant glimmer that blazed in her consciousness. Still, she forced herself to lie, denying the power of the Dreamtime in her words, despite the truth in her heart.

"Grandfather's just an old man. He thinks he can tell the future, talking about crusaders coming to stop you. All I get is him, and he goes back on his word to keep me safe."

"I tried, kiddo," Bolan apologized. He stepped forward and Yin pressed Wangara to the wall behind him, the pistol almost out of his waistband.

"Wait," Yeung said.

Bolan nodded, and he mouthed "good job" to his two young companions. Yin and Wangara were confused. He'd played out the drama, getting Wangara to sell her worth to Yeung. Yin's belief in the teen, and his willingness to protect her was icing on the cake.

"No money?" Yeung asked.

Wangara raised her hands. "Don't want to be your problem."

Yin settled the gun back in its spot on his waistband, and he wrapped one slender arm around her narrow shoulders. "I'll take care of everything, right?"

Wangara looked up, realizing that Yin's gentle, one-armed hug was genuine, full of concern and affection. She smiled weakly. "Sure."

"Young love. You can't break that up," Bolan said with a tilt of his head.

"So where is he?" Yeung asked with resignation.

"Grandfather has a few hideouts. The night your boys burned down our house, we were in a lean-to a hundred yards away, watching the whole place go up," Wangara said. "But that's not his only place. He has a sweat lodge built of mud. And then there are the Uluru caves."

"There are hundreds of them," Yeung groaned.

"Yeah, but he took me to some," the young woman said.

"So why'd you run?" Yeung asked.

She raised an eyebrow.

"If you didn't go for help—"

"If I were going for help, I'd have taken a bus to Sydney and spoke with the authorities," she explained. "I was going to Darwin to throw myself on your mercy. I didn't realize you were in my backyard."

"How'd you think we were in Darwin?" Yeung asked.

"Port city plus close to China, it's simple math, even for an Abo," Wangara said, the final phrase said with mocking emphasis. "Not all of us living on the reservation are primitive screw-heads."

"How deep are these caves?" Bolan asked.

"Some are practically mazes," Wangara answered. "A few are interlinked. He keeps camping supplies in them."

"He have any guns?" Yeung asked.

Wangara nodded. "He's not supposed to…"

Yeung laughed, patting the silver Beretta hanging in his shoulder holster. "Right. No one in Australia is supposed to be armed."

Wangara shrugged. "He was part of an Australian unit that served as observers in Southeast Asia. He's got a few souvenirs from way back when."

"A few?" Yeung asked.

"One of those rifles with the banana-shaped clips," she said. "A couple of black rifles with handles on top. A shotgun. A .45, and a couple other pistols I don't know."

"An AK and some M-16s," Bolan said. "Pretty impressive."

"Grandfather believed trouble was coming," Wangara said. "But then, he was watching too many *Mad Max* movies, if you know what I mean."

Yeung chuckled. "Know where this cave is?"

"Not on a map, but from my house, I could lead you there," Wangara explained.

Bolan nodded to Yeung. "Every hunter needs a good guide."

"You've got your hunting gear?" Yeung asked.

"In the SUV, a duffel in the trunk," Bolan informed him.

Yeung nodded to one bodyguard. "Have someone pick up his bag. We're heading back to the facility."

"Why not drive?" Bolan asked.

"Because it's near a thousand damn miles, and I've got a helicopter," Yeung responded.

"Helicopters don't have that kind of range," Bolan admonished.

Yeung rolled his eyes. "I'm exaggerating. The chopper has the range. I want this done and over with. The sooner we get to the facility, the sooner I can start the expansion. The sooner the expansion's done, the sooner I go home to sweet old Hong Kong."

Bolan nodded. "That sounds perfect."

The Executioner was all for anything putting him in the facility. With Wangara's informed leading and Yin's unintentional aid, he'd been able to play with Yeung's perceptions. He'd arranged for her safety in a roundabout manner, in fact arranging for Wangara to get out of ground zero and right into her grandfather's stronghold.

Not everything was perfect. Bolan didn't want to go up against Yin in a conflict, but he was fairly certain that Yeung would keep him on as the Black Rose's liaison with their Hong Kong–based assassin. The Executioner only had to convince Yin that the destruction of the facility was a worthwhile goal and going against the triad could be a winning proposition. This way, he could get Yin away from the anvil that Frankie Law's crew of vengeance-seekers intended to hammer.

Turning Yin fully to the side of angels would be difficult, but even if that were accomplished, Bolan still had Yeung's forces, Law's loyal gangsters and Garrett Victor's solitary survivor at large to deal with. If he somehow managed to end the Black Rose civil war in Australia and destroy the facility, taking out the last mercenary, there was still one dangling thread.

The treacherous Eugene Waylon, in Hong Kong, still had to be accounted for.

The road would be smooth for Bolan, at least for a short stretch, but sooner or later, it was going to return to the Executioner's usual game of blood and thunder. Fortunately, in the middle of the outback, in the shadow of Ayers Rock, there was plenty of room for Bolan's cleansing flames to burn without scorching a single innocent bystander.

FRANKIE LAW FLICKED his lighter, then paused, seeing the man in the motorcycle leathers strolling toward his truck.

Law let the tongue of flame burn out, the filter dropping from his lips. He didn't like the look of the man, especially with the frame of the pistol so obvious in his waistband under his jacket's open lapels. Instead of reaching for the handgun, though, the man fished a lighter from his pocket, firing it up.

"Need a light?" Lucenzo asked.

Law put the cigarette between his lips and puffed until the end glowed as a bright orange ember. He let smoke drift from his nostrils. "Who're you?"

"A friend," Lucenzo said, putting the lighter away. He made no effort to hide his Beretta.

"I don't have many white friends," Law returned. "And none of them look like you."

"I'm just a friend you haven't met yet. John Lucenzo, sent here to kill the guy posing as the Black Rose's assassin," the mercenary explained.

"What?" Law asked. "Posing?"

"You've been suckered," Lucenzo explained. "Guys like you don't back down, they just regather and hit back hard."

"How do you know me?" Law asked. "And how would I know you?"

"Because I was hired to kill the guy," Lucenzo told him. "And I've been listening to the news. Actually, the guy paying me has heard all of this news. How it seemed like there might have been a squabble in the Australian territories owned by the Black Rose, and you're Frankie Law, the guy who's been running their business out here until Bobby Yeung moved in."

"That so?" Law bristled. The whine of a helicopter rose behind the hotel.

Lucenzo jerked his thumb toward the sound. "That's Bobby Yeung flying back to his homestead, with a guy he thinks he's hired to clean out some problems with a land deal."

"And you know the truth?" Law fumed as he realized the men he'd come to kill were flying off. The Bell Jet-Ranger rose into the sky, peeling off toward the facility in the shadow of Ayers Rock. "Smart man. So why are you coming to me?"

Lucenzo looked around. "You see anyone with me?"

"No."

"He drew me off with a distraction and killed the heart of my team. Thing is, I need to be paid. And the guy who hired me, he doesn't want anyone to know that his meal ticket is a corpse, and someone came here in his place," Lucenzo said.

"So you're trolling for a job yourself," Law mused. "You come to me. We become friends. With me as your contact, you can go back to Waylon and say you're the new man."

Lucenzo smirked. "You know Eugene."

"He's my main contact, or was my main contact when I needed to hire the Black Rose assassin," Law stated. "It didn't take much to figure out he was our boy's cohort. Business manager or accountant, or just the guy who knows who to hire when it comes time to replace a hurt or worn-out op. You impress him, you'll be the new go-to guy," Law said.

"I bring you to him, he'll be really impressed," Lucenzo said. "And you'll need someone who can give you some tactical help, to take down Yeung, and to outthink this guy."

"We've got him outnumbered and outgunned," Law replied.

"Bet you were ready for him last time and had a ton of guns and guys," Lucenzo answered. "But you end up with a fire gutting your offices and a dozen corpses."

Law narrowed his eyes.

"I'm right," Lucenzo said.

"Right. A match made in hell," Law grumbled. "You think you can help me out?"

"I'm sure this guy's a military vet. That makes him partially predictable," Lucenzo answered. "There are specific responses to certain threat situations for a military mind, but considering this guy's probably seen more unconventional combat, we're talking playing hard and dirty. I think that between the two of us, we can come up with something that'll throw him a mind fuck that can kill."

Law thought about Lucenzo's offer for a moment, then a smile crossed his face slowly, the first honest smile he'd felt since Ton's death. It wasn't happiness, but the malicious mirth was a good substitute.

"I like your way with words," Law said. "Let's throw that little party."

12

When the Executioner finally got his first glance at the facility, he was dismayed at the sheer scope of it. There was a full-sized, low-topped complex, its roof patterned with camouflage that disguised it from faster-moving, higher-flying aircraft. Only the fact that the Bell JetRanger was flying up on it from close range and eyes sharp enough to penetrate the optical illusion of terrain patterning on a flat surface from an angle enabled him to see the extent of it. Bolan could tell that he was looking at a 250,000-square-foot blockhouse, akin to the kinds of structures he'd noticed at covert military development installations. The runways were also similarly patterned in sheets of camouflage paint. There were skid marks along the runways where the wheels of transport planes had scuffed them away, but rather than make the runways more obvious from up high, they would simply blend in as natural-looking ruts.

There were shacks and tents spread out, their roofs adorned with netting that rendered them indistinguishable from the natural rough scrub present in the outback. Off to the sides of the runways were various aircraft, each with camouflage tarps over them.

"Like what you don't see?" Yeung asked, elbowing Bolan in the side.

"I see quite a bit, but that's just me. Anyone else wouldn't know this was here unless they knew it like the back of their hand," Bolan replied. "Excellent setup."

"We had a few advisers on what we needed to do. Nothing is too tall down there, so it won't show up as a major disruption in the normally flat terrain," Yeung said. "The blockhouse is a quarter of a million square feet. We can store nearly a kiloton of heroin in one corner, and I intend to begin the process of digging a proper storage cellar."

"All this is just for storing heroin?" Bolan asked.

"We also handle other forms of contraband. The nice thing about being out here, the air is dry and it's not too hot or cold," Yeung replied. "Stolen and knocked-off electronics keep nicely here. We had a crew intercept a freighter from Japan, and they're going to bring in a few thousand high-definition plasma-screen TVs among other things."

"That's a lot of profit," Bolan admitted. "How about weapons?"

"We've got brand-new, freshly delivered to Russian troops AK-107's. Buy them off a general for a few rubles apiece, and then sell them and their brand-new 5.45 mm ammo to the highest bidder. We've got a cartel in Colombia looking for a couple thousand rifles and five million rounds of ammo. Sounds like the FARC is looking to kick it up a notch if you ask me. At our price, we make a damn good profit."

Bolan nodded. The helicopter swung around the block-house, and he could make out conical vents poking up from the roof, concentrated mainly in one corner. "Lot of ventilation there."

"We've got a section devoted to cutting the heroin for street distribution. We do it here, so there's less chance of trouble when it hits the streets," Yeung said. "That's the only problem with this place—when it's cooking, you can smell it for miles."

"Which is a good thing that you're miles from no-where," Bolan said.

Yeung shrugged. "Except for the fucking Abos. They get all uptight because they can smell us."

"And you're using sacred land to brew your poison," Wangara spoke up.

Yeung raised an eyebrow. "You're going to give me trouble about this now?"

She shook her head. "No, sir. I'm just saying why Grandfather and his friends have their loincloths in a bunch. Me, I intend to have a quiet little apartment, cable and a good Internet hookup, thanks to my new boyfriend."

Yin chuckled and Yeung winked at his employee. "I know how to pick 'em, right?"

Bolan's face bent into a smile he didn't feel as he continued to study the layout. The blockhouse was huge, with few entrances. He knew he was going to be hard-pressed to develop an effective combat strategy. His MP-5 and Desert Eagle had been left behind in Alice Springs, so his problems were going to be more difficult. The VEPR was an excellent long-range modification of a traditional close-quarters weapon, but its willowy, long barrel would limit its maneuverability in tight quarters. "How many men does it take to run a place like this?" he asked.

"I've got a hundred, plus the crews of the planes that come in," Yeung replied. "Though, most of them are locals. We displaced a dozen poachers when we set up shop, but when they found out we were looking for someone who wasn't afraid of busting a cap in an Abo's ass, or arse as they like to say here, we got about forty people."

Bolan raised his eyebrows, showing appeciation that didn't extend further than feeding Yeung's burgeoning ego. The Executioner realized that this was a truly amazing setup, a contraband transport hub and secret airport enabling the triads to spread their smuggling efficiency across the globe. This would be the first such facility of its kind. The triads already owned China's airports, or at least major portions of them, but their international control was lacking. Privately owned airstrips were one thing, but the facility also had processing capacity as well as storage for tons of contraband that didn't have to go through bribed Chinese customs officials. Of course, the Black Rose Triad would expect its own excise tax of the other triads for using this facility, but the rival Chinese gangs were used to dealing with one another. The Black Rose Triad was only one of many, and they bartered and worked together often in a semblance of civility that underscored their competitive natures. The facility would ingratiate the Black Rose with some, and antagonize others, but all would respect their industrious initiative and pay their dues.

The race would be on, though, to set up other hubs in remote locations. Bolan surmised that potential hot spots would be in Africa and South America, and potentially the Middle East. With the Chinese presence in Africa and Panama, it wouldn't be hard to imagine a potential war between triads for such control. These facilities would also provide forward clearing bases for Communist Chinese government agents to move even more discreetly than usual.

The Executioner needed to nip this in the bud before the triads expanded their operations to a staggering global level. The JetRanger landed on a small helipad. Even as Bolan, Yeung, Yin and Wangara disembarked, the flight crew rolled it off to the side, throwing camouflage netting over it so it would blend in with the surrounding scrub. He could see it, but only because he was a few yards away and on the ground.

"How were you able to do all this construction without being noticed?" Bolan asked.

Yeung chuckled. "We spent a lot of money, but we were able to hide a lot of this by disguising it as a major archaeological expedition. We greased enough palms in the Northern Territory government to hide it all."

"The blockhouse?" Bolan asked.

"Prefabricated building materials we were able to assemble here," Yeung said. He rapped a wall. The metallic clatter was evident. "Same stuff as Quonset huts. It can handle the weather really well, because this place is just so mild. We've been working five years on this. We only just finished the processing part of the facility five months ago."

"This must have cost a lot," Bolan grumbled.

"Five hundred million," Yeung admitted. "But we've made it all back in savings on transport costs."

"Five years?" Bolan asked. "Hell of a long time for a gamble. They only just started acting up?"

"First it was the processing chemical fumes, but we're going to start major digging and the Aboriginals we'd added on to do the excavation for the underground tunnels got uptight and went to their leaders," Yeung explained. "Then things got really tense. We've paid off or beat up most of the opposition, but some fuckers just need to die, get it?"

"Oh, I understand," Bolan said. "Don't worry. Everyone who needs to die, will."

Yeung grinned, not realizing that the Executioner had just declared his death sentence.

LUCENZO FOLLOWED Frankie Law's convoy on his motorcycle. He was glad to have an actual guide on hand to lead him out into the middle of nowhere. There was no way that he could have kept up with the helicopter. Even if he had given pursuit on the bike, he would have kicked up so much dirt he would have been noticed, Yeung's security force expecting him and firing from a mile away. Even if his quarry, the big killer in black, wasn't part of the equation, there was no way that Lucenzo could have taken on all those odds, no matter how much firepower he had.

Lucenzo and Law sat perched just behind the crest of a hill, observing the sprawl of the facility through binoculars.

"So, what are we going to do?" Law asked.

"How many people does he have on hand?" Lucenzo asked.

"Yeung brought in his own people from Hong Kong,"

Law explained. "He picked up others from the ranks of local poachers and outback yahoos."

Lucenzo raised an eyebrow. "How many?"

"He's got about one hundred men down there, give or take a dozen," Law stated. "That's not counting the flight crews of aircraft that come in to drop off or pick up contraband. It's hard to tell, thanks to the camouflage netting, but there's about a half-dozen aircraft on the side."

Lucenzo scanned the lumps, making out the outlines of at least three tail booms towering nearly thirty feet into the air. He gave a low whistle and looked to Law. "You've got transport jets down there?"

"Yeung does. I don't have it," Law said, taking a moment's pause. "Yet."

Lucenzo nodded. "So, that's another part of the reason you're here personally."

"That's a tasty slice of pie, and I want it," Law grumbled. "Why shouldn't I be running it? I've run Australia for the Black Rose for ten years."

"You'll get it. We'll just let our opponents do all the work," Lucenzo replied. "You told me that this killer told you to lay low, that he was going to clear the way for you, right?"

"But you said he was baiting me to come after Yeung and him," Law said.

Lucenzo smirked. "This guy used you to establish his street cred with Yeung. Call him up."

Law's eyes widened. "But he'll—"

"Take a look," Lucenzo interrupted. He pointed toward a small prefab shack. Two ATVs, one with the American and the teenage girl, the other with Yin, rolled out, seen off by Bobby Yeung and his bodyguards.

"He'll know that his assassin isn't working for him," Law stated. "Yeung'll be fired up for that guy, and throw everyone he has at him."

"Trust me, if this guy plowed through two dozen of your boys in close-quarters combat, just imagine how devastating he'd be having uneven terrain for cover and a long-range rifle?" Lucenzo asked. "Take a look. It looks like he's got a Dragunov sniper rifle."

"Dragunov?" Law asked.

"A really powerful sniper version of the AK," Lucenzo explained. "Even if it's not, that thing has a scope made for killing targets to almost a mile out."

"It'd be a hundred against three. He's not going to take out that many of Yeung's people," Law said.

"Even if he doesn't, he'll cut the odds down much more in our favor," Lucenzo said. "And who knows, he might even be able to obliterate Yeung's people. We'd have a cakewalk against one man, worn down by taking down a hundred to one odds."

Law looked at the ATVs rolling toward the Uluru mound, doubt dulling his features. "He takes down a hundred guys, and we hit him with a quarter of that force and expect to win?"

"We focus on him," Lucenzo said. "Flank, use our brains and superior numbers and tactical use of terrain. The same stuff he'll use to obliterate Yeung's people."

"And you're so certain that one guy has that kind of edge?" Law asked.

"He wiped out your boys. He took advantage of the

terrain, used your own people as shields against each other, and utilized surprise and lateral movement. He'll do the same thing on a larger scale, using even more surprise and movement skills and precision firepower," Lucenzo observed. "This is a guy who thinks his way around combat, looking for the holes in his opponents' armor. He's already seen the main facility. He's got a good layout. He'll drop off the girl, maybe snuff the mook Yeung sent with him, and come back alone."

Law's eyes narrowed. "Yeah, 'cause the little mook isn't worth shit."

"Hey, just speculating what might happen," Lucenzo stated. "Nothing personal. Throw Yeung the bone, and let's watch the bullets fly."

Law took out his phone, glaring at Lucenzo. He hit the speed dial, watching through his binoculars as Yeung fished his own phone out of his jacket. "Hey, Bobby, guess who's alive, and guess who's been fucking you over?"

On the other side of the binoculars, even from a mile away, he could see the rage boiling off the Black Rose Triad boss.

"YOU OKAY THERE, Bobby bro?" Frankie Law chided over the cell phone. "You're not talking."

"You're alive," Yeung said, struggling to control his rage. He squeezed the phone, hearing its shell crack as he held on to it. "Who were the bodies?"

"My people, old chum," Law answered. "And I owe you big-time. But I figure I'd let the two who screwed me have it out and come looking for me."

Yeung closed his eyes, sucking in a deep breath, then letting it out slowly.

"Anger issues, buddy?" Law asked.

"I'm going to kill you," Yeung pronounced. "And when you die, it's not going to be fast and easy. It's not going to be a bullet in the head. It's going to be by the knife."

Law laughed. "Hey, you have to deal with that guy who says he's your assassin. He told me I could live if I laid low until after he wiped you out. He knows where you live." Law hung up.

Yeung looked around. "All right! We're on full alert! Anyone sees Stone, shoot him dead. Get me a crew of poachers, because I'm sending a squad out after him. He pulled one over on me, and no one fucks with Bobby Yeung. *No one!*"

He hurled the cell phone against the wall, shattering it. He watched the broken plastic pieces fall like his broken hopes. Everything had gone out of control.

THE HONDA FourTrax Recon ATVs were powerful machines with engines that would give the roughest dirt bike a run for its money. Despite having a two-wheel-drive transmission, they were still able to traverse rough terrain at a ground-eating pace. Even so, they'd only been travelling for fifteen minutes from the facility when Bolan glanced in the mirror, seeing a distant cloud forming in their wake.

The Executioner could guess what had happened. Law, in a play to even the odds with Yeung, had probably revealed his identity. It was nothing that Bolan hadn't anticipated. In fact, he'd hoped that Law would try to use the information, so as to force Yeung's hand and give away the element of surprise. The Executioner had been prepared for trouble from the start, his reflexes wound like springs, ready to snap when the Black Rose mobsters made their move. He looked over to Yin who had also seen the dust trail.

"I thought that we were supposed to do this alone," Yin called over the low buzz of their engines.

Bolan held up his hand to inform the young triad man to stop so they could converse a little more easily. Though the engines were quiet, he still knew the news he had to drop was better said face-to-face instead of shouted across a distance. He was going to take a chance, and from what he'd seen of the young man's loyalty to his wounded friend, and his willingness to step between Yeung and Wangara, he knew his bet would be relatively safe. If it wasn't, he still had the Walther resting in its shoulder holster.

Yin pulled to a halt next to Bolan and Wangara. "What's going on?" he asked.

"Yeung found out that I'm not the man he hired," Bolan explained.

A moment of shock registered on the young Chinese man's face as the information hit him like a ton of bricks. He looked down, seeing the butt of a Ruger Mini-14 poking out of a saddle sheath on his ATV. Yin turned back to Bolan and Wangara, and shrugged.

"I guess neither am I," Yin said. "Bobby lost my loyalty when he made her disposable."

Wangara reached out, putting her hand on his shoulder. "Thank you. I know it's not going to be easy for you."

"Don't worry about it," Yin replied. "Maybe your grandfather won't mind if I shack up with you folks for a while."

"Think it'll be safe for you here?" Bolan inquired.

"You're here to take out the facility, right? And you've taken out Law and are going to bring down Yeung. Who's going to be left gunning for me?" Yin asked.

Bolan took a deep breath. "Law's not dead yet."

Yin nodded, digesting the information. He looked up and smiled. "*Yet*. But I've seen you operate. Yet's only three letters between you and all my troubles going away. And if you want—"

"I've got it. I need someone to look after Arana," Bolan explained. "You don't mind sitting on the sidelines, do you?"

Yin looked back. "With the hornet's nest you've stirred up, there's definitely not going to be a safe spot anywhere between here and Alice Springs. Arana needs the protection."

"Then let's go. The enemy's eating up our lead time," Bolan warned.

Yin fired up his ATV and joined the Executioner as they rocketed toward Grandfather Wangara.

OBWE WANGARA STOOD at the entrance of his cave, a Colt .45 tucked into his waistband at the small of his back, and an AK-47 leaning against a rock at the mouth of the tunnel. He lowered the binoculars. He'd seen the man from the Dreamtime, his granddaughter's arms wrapped around his chest. A young Chinese man was riding alongside him on an ATV, and even farther back, the specks of a squadron of Australian poachers on similar vehicles.

He'd earned the nickname Grandfather because of his link with his ancestors through his meditative trances. The world was full of coincidences, but there was no way mere happenstance could have explained away the similarity of the man Arana was riding with and the vision that had come to him. All those years ago, when he'd been in Southeast Asia, he'd made his first contact with the Dreamtime when he'd suffered his first gunshot wound. Absently, he traced the scar tissue on his stomach, remembering what he'd originally believed were morphine-induced hallucinations of old Aboriginal shamen appearing to him, granting him the strength to survive a 7.62 mm slug that had torn out a four-inch section of his bowel.

He'd lived, and the power of his ancestors had been passed on to him, guiding him through life. He'd discovered a daughter he'd sired before he'd went off with the military, finding her on her last legs of life. He was there for her, helping her to survive long enough to deliver Arana before she succumbed to fatal liver damage. He'd taken care of the girl, and now, she was bringing him help.

The Chinese man with them gave him some trouble, but Wangara trusted the man his ancestors had sent to him. What was more disturbing was the group of men pursuing them.

Wangara folded his arms, knowing that the Chinese triad had unleashed their hounds on the crusader. For the time being, they were out of range of his AK-47, and even if he could take a shot, his granddaughter was in the way, potentially in the path of a cross fire. He'd have to bide his time, and so he closed his eyes, feeling his consciousness expand.

Rising into the Dreamtime, he immediately saw the storm looming on the horizon, thick clouds of turmoil rolling across the outback, threatening to smother the entire countryside. The conflict had its roots in the facility just south of the great Uluru mound, but this was only a lightning rod, and the blazing spear of sky fire had tracked from the Great Water all the way down through the Northern Territory, threatening to burn his eyes out with the great light it carried. The choking gloom that had shrouded his land was split by its path.

The lightning was the path of the mystery man.

"That is justice," the voices of his ancestors said. "Justice made flesh, come for its purpose."

Wangara opened his eyes as the thrum of ATV motors grew stronger. The two vehicles pulled to a halt and Arana leaped from her seat, running to him, her skinny arms wrapping around him.

"Grandfather Wangara, I presume?" Bolan asked, sliding off the saddle-style seat. He kept his hands open and by his sides, making no threatening movements. Yin did the same.

"Obwe Wangara," he introduced himself.

"Your granddaughter told me you were expecting me," Bolan said.

"The crusader," Wangara admitted, nodding to him.

Yin introduced himself. "You can trust me, Grandfather," he said.

Wangara looked him over, as if he could peer through the layers of the young triad fugitive to see deep into his soul. That penetrating gaze found no menace in his heart. "I believe you. What about them?"

Bolan turned, looking at the dust cloud on the horizon. Because the trailing dust of his own passage couldn't have been minimized, it was as if a neon arrow were aimed at the cave. He drew the heavy-caliber VEPR. "I've got everything under control. Get into the cave and take cover," Bolan ordered.

Yin took out his Ruger, and the old man handed Arana his Colt .45, picking up his AK-47.

"If it comes this far, they won't have an easy time," Wangara said. "Good luck, warrior."

Bolan nodded and took off toward a sniper's roost he'd chosen. He didn't want to insult the Aboriginal shaman by telling him that luck would have nothing to do with the outcome of this battle.

Only decades of battle experience, intense mental conditioning and a few minutes of preparation.

The Executioner nestled atop a dune, preparing to call down thunder on Yeung's hired guns.

13

Angus MacEwan rode at the lead of the group, a Winchester Model 70 bolt-action rifle bouncing against his back, his goggles and helmet protecting his face from kicked-up dust as he plowed across the outback. The Winchester had served him well during his job as poacher, and he was able to hit a wallaby from three hundred meters with the hunting rifle. He knew full well that the terrain needed more than the stubby, short-range chatterboxes the Chinese gangsters were armed with. The squadron of ATVs was about a kilometer from the base of the Uluru mound when he heard the first crack of a rifle. MacEwan watched as one of his handlebars splintered on impact. A sudden lurch of the ATV saved his life as the vehicle absorbed the high-velocity bullet that was intended for his heart.

MacEwan threw himself off the ATV, rolling in the dirt, howling for the others to take cover. One of his fellow poachers, a hulk of a man named Roberts, jerked violently as his hat rocketed off his head atop a geyser of spewing blood.

"Take cover!" MacEwan repeated. He scurried to the

upended ATV and wrestled his Winchester loose. Another .300 Winchester Magnum round sizzled, careening off the frame of the ATV and screaming off into the sky. The poacher curled up tightly, expecting another bullet to spear through the air. It did, but the fourth rifle shot wasn't aimed at him. It punched into the heart of a scrawny little rag of a man who was pulling out a Remington semiauto pump rifle. He folded, the Remington clattering to the dirt on one side of his ATV while he flopped over the other side.

Two men dead out of the dozen he'd brought with him, and his own ATV was a twisted mass of wreckage. Whatever Stone was shooting, he was taking shots quickly and accurately, faster and surer than if he'd been cutting loose with a bolt-action. Another man howled as he took a bullet through the shoulder, and a second ATV nose-dived into the dirt as a high-velocity, heavy slug shattered its front-end fork, rendering it out of control.

Its rider tumbled next to MacEwan, one leg twisted in a knot of shattered bone and torn muscle, and his face was gouged, pouring blood from where he'd smashed into a rock. Butler was the poacher's name, and he clawed at MacEwan's sleeve.

"It hurts! It hurts!"

"Shut up!" MacEwan snapped. He whipped the wooden stock of his Winchester hard across the man's jaw, shattering it. "Try shouting now, you stupid little bitch!"

The VEPR belched out rocketing bullets at the speed of sound. MacEwan respected the kind of precision shooting that Stone had opened up with. A fifth poacher spun as his shoulder vomited an explosion of splintered bone and pulpy tissue.

The wounded man moaned in despair, the volume of his groan for aid, dropping off as ruptured arteries gushed his life into puddles of crimson. MacEwan watched the man, whose name he couldn't recall, expire within the space of a few seconds. He threw the bolt on his Winchester, chambering a .308 cartridge, and from behind the cover of the overturned ATV, he intended to take out the assassin. From the trajectory of the gunshots, he had an estimate of the sniper position, but before he could focus through his scope, he felt a searing pain in his thigh. MacEwan looked back to see the sniveling Butler draw back his bloody knife to stab him again. The poacher whipped the Winchester around and shoved the end of the rifle's barrel into Butler's mouth, folding his broken jaw to the right. MacEwan pulled the trigger and kicked the corpse to one side.

He turned back in time to see a speck rocketing toward him. Before MacEwan could register the tiny blur, it struck him on the bridge of his nose.

THE EXECUTIONER NAILED the triad's hired point man between the eyes, but he didn't have time to celebrate as the enemy survivors cut loose with their hunting rifles. He slithered off the crest of the dune and scrambled toward another vantage point he'd picked out before he started the battle. Bullets ripped through the air at supersonic speed, their passage breaking the atmosphere with loud cracks. The poachers' muzzle-blasts came along as distant thumps a second after the high-velocity projectiles.

Bolan dumped his VEPR's magazine on the run, slamming home a spare. He'd burned off the first twenty rounds, taking out half of the twelve-man death squad sent after him, dividing his fire between destroying ATVs and taking down imminent threats. Throwing himself prone atop his secondary sniper's roost, he targeted the man trying to rally the remaining gunmen. A 175-grain hollowpoint round leaped across the thousand-yard range, bleeding off a third of its velocity before it struck the newly promoted leader in his open, shouting mouth.

Bolan had intended to put the shot an inch higher, right in the man's triangle to spare him any suffering through complete destruction of his central nervous system. As it was, the shot merely vaporized the trunk of the gunman's spine. He collapsed like a rag doll into the dirt, left quadriplegic for the few moments it took for him to suffocate as his lungs no longer received the nerve impulses that spurred them to take in breath. Sightless eyes stared back through Bolan's scope in the moment before he swung to acquire a new target.

One of the poachers decided to try to charge the Executioner's position and hopped back onto his ATV, revving it to full speed, skipping across the sand. Bolan swung the VEPR, triggering four shots, trying to catch up with the weaving ATV. On his fifth round, he caught the hardcharger through his left shoulder. The distance was only six hundred yards at that point, so the .300 Magnum bullet hadn't slowed down much. It hit the joint of the poacher's shoulder and burrowed deep, plowing through his collarbone like a supersonic drill. The cavernous tunnel of destruction wrought in the Magnum round's passage severed brachial arteries and the ATV rider's windpipe.

The ATV spun out from under the lifeless man, launching off a dune and doing a flip before it collapsed in a mangled mash of metal and fiberglass. The corpse bounced, limbs flailing as it tumbled to a halt in a less spectacular fashion.

A quick sweep of the battlefield and Bolan noticed that the leader of the group had killed one of his own, leaving only three active combatants opposing him.

The number dropped to two as one hopped on his ATV and wheeled back toward the facility at full speed, kicking up clouds of dust.

One of the Australian roughnecks wielding a monster .458 Magnum hunting rifle stood his ground, hammering out a sky-splitting slug that landed a foot short of the Executioner's position. The divot of earth thrown up by the 400-grain missile was indicative of the devastation it would have wrought on Bolan's body. The .458 was designed for taking down big animals such as wildebeest and lions at close range. Only its massive weight had kept it from staying aloft long enough to hit Bolan, but the burly rifleman was adjusting, raising his aim to compensate for bullet-drop. Bolan cut him off with a shot that split his heart in two.

Bolan ducked as a .308 Winchester round chopped the top of the mound of dirt he'd hidden behind. Dust sprayed down on his shoulders as he retreated to his third fire position, shooting on the move. He wasn't running as much as he was taking long, steady strides where he could pause and trigger the rifle.

The last rifleman was tucked deep behind his broken-down ATV, kept under cover by the Magnum slugs smashing into the ATV. As long as the bullets plunked into the wrecked frame, Bolan's final opponent wouldn't be able to draw a bead on him.

The Executioner decided to let the rifleman finish the battle himself and held his fire and ground for the space of five seconds. The gunman popped up from behind cover to look for Bolan and exposed his head as a picture-perfect target. Bolan took advantage of the man's tactical mistake and used a single round to chop the dome of his skull off from midforehead.

As soon as the conflict had started, it was over.

Bolan reloaded the VEPR and pocketed his partially spent magazine. He plucked his phone from its pocket and called Bobby Yeung on speed dial. It took a few moments to connect as the phone had to be forwarded to a new unit. The triad boss had to have been pushed close to the edge that he had destroyed one of his cell phones in a fit of frustration.

"Stone?" Yeung asked.

"The one and only," Bolan replied.

"Let me guess. You're not calling to surrender," the Black Rose boss said.

"You've got one coming back to the roost. He was smart. The others, they didn't live long enough to learn any lessons," Bolan taunted. "Maybe you could learn a thing or two."

"Like what? How to be a coward?" Yeung asked.

Bolan sighed. "How to die of old age in your bed. But it was just a thought. You want to die in a blaze of glory, I'll be happy to do that for you."

"Fuck off and die, Stone," Yeung snapped. "I'll piss on your grave! Law is here. If we don't get you, he will."

"Who do you think invited him to this little party?" Bolan asked. "You think I wanted either of you still standing when I left Australia? It doesn't matter if you're at each other's throats or united against me. I'll kill you, and go on with my life. It's what I do, and I'm very good at it."

"Stone, we can make a deal then," Yeung said.

"Good. Burn it all down and run with your tail between your legs," Bolan suggested.

"Fuck off," Yeung countered.

"Shame. You seemed so reasonable," Bolan said, hanging up. He'd undercut the mob boss's confidence. Even though he still possessed eighty-to-one odds against the Executioner, he was willing to suggest compromise.

When it came to organized crime leaders, Bolan believed the only compromise involved their choice of caskets if they refused to unconditionally surrender.

OBWE WANGARA WAITED at the mouth of the cave as Bolan rejoined his charges.

"You handled that well," Wangara complimented.

Bolan shrugged. "It's only the opening shots. Are you all going to be okay here?"

"We've got a complication or two," Wangara said.

Bolan's eyes narrowed. "The reason you were waiting at the mouth of the cave with an arsenal when we first came."

"More or less," Wangara answered. "Follow me."

Bolan did so, following the Aboriginal shaman through the twisting tunnels adorned with wall paintings that stretched thousands of years into humankind's ancient history. The Uluru mound's cave systems were full of them, the first signs of civilization in Australia, a tangible record of primitive man's ability to record memories in permanent form. The scrawls on the walls betrayed the importance of what Wangara was fighting for.

These lands were the birthright of his people, and evidence of who they were. Instead of being mere savages, they were a culture older than even the Chinese, with a history stretching across aeons, literally written in stone. This was the kind of fight that exemplified the Executioner's reason for being, protecting the things that really mattered to people. The Aboriginal tribes had struggled long and hard in the Australian courts in order to regain full custody of their ancestral lands. For the triads to annex this for the purposes of drug and gun smuggling was an insult to a people who had resorted not to violence, but civilized discourse.

Bolan followed Wangara into a chamber and saw Yin and Arana bracketing a burly man in a sheriff's uniform, a dark splotch on his forehead.

"Sheriff Ansen Crown, meet Mr. Stone," Wangara said. "Crown came poking around and found my hideout. He took a bruising, but he's all right."

Bolan looked at the bound sheriff. "He was looking for you? But not out of concern."

"Yeung gave me two choices. Money in my pocket, or he'd cut off my children's feet," Crown said. "What would you take?"

"Untie him," Bolan ordered.

"He's working for Yeung," Wangara said.

Bolan locked eyes with Crown. "Only under duress. If he acts up too much, I'll deal with the problem," he said.

Crown's eyes widened. "He said he'd mutilate my kids! He has them at that fucking place!"

"Where?" Bolan asked.

"He has them in a storage area, surrounded by chemical drums," Crown explained. "They were marked inflammable. Please—"

Bolan nodded. "Sit still and behave. I'll bring your kids back."

"That was the complication," Wangara said. "Yeung has hostages at the facility. My ancestors told me that you wouldn't risk the lives of children."

"Your ancestors have good intel," Bolan replied.

"You believe my ancestors have explained to me about you?" Wangara asked.

Bolan shrugged, remembering more incidents of greater-than-human perception across his career. "I've experienced stranger. So you tied up Crown not out of spite."

"But to protect him from himself. He runs off trying to save his kids, he might get them killed," Wangara said.

"You'd do any better?" Crown asked, rubbing his raw wrists.

Bolan glared at the sheriff for a long moment. Nothing needed to be said, and Crown cringed from the intensity of the Executioner's hard blue eyes. The sheriff eventually cleared his throat. "You need pictures?"

"Just their names. I don't think there are too many kids in a major drug processing lab," Bolan said. He took a deep breath and looked to Yin.

"Sidekick time?" the ex-triad soldier asked. "Someone's going to have to bring those tykes back here."

"I'll have to come, too," Arana said. "He said kids, and there's only room for two on each of these ATVs."

"You just got back here to safety," Grandfather Wangara protested.

Arana glared him. "What was it you said? I'm not a child anymore. But children's lives *are* at stake!"

"What about me?" Crown asked. "They're my children."

"You've got a head injury and are not a hundred percent," Bolan told him. "Plus, you've been restrained for a while. Your mobility is compromised. We'll need speed and stealth to get the kids out, and with your authority, you'll be the only one who can bring in help."

"Help?" Crown asked.

Bolan nodded. "There's a lot of material in the facility that shouldn't fall into the wrong hands, and I won't be able to take care of it all. We need professional help. Grandfather, you have to go with him."

"They've got others on the payroll," Crown warned.

"You know who will stonewall you because they've got triad money in their pockets?" Bolan inquired. "Rat them out then. You've got the pull necessary. I'll get your kids to safety. And I'll cover Arana and Yin when they get the kids out of the facility."

Bolan handed Crown his satellite phone and gave his VEPR to Wangara. "This is just like your AK-47. Same operation, except it doesn't do full-auto. It has a longer reach. You'll need the range."

The Executioner looked over Wangara's arsenal. Except for a pouch of old Soviet-era stick grenades and spare ammunition for both of his assault rifles, the cave was primarily equipped with food and necessities for a long stay in the caves. There was also a Lee Enfield Mk-IV that Arana immediately picked up. She stuffed a couple of 10-round stripper clips into a pouch and shouldered that.

"How good are you?" Bolan asked.

"Been shooting razorbacks for five years," she answered. She threw back the bolt, jammed a stripper clip into the open breech and pushed the 10-round load down into the integral magazine. She discarded the clip and slammed the breech shut in a single motion. "Razorbacks are tough and fast. And I can work the bolt as fast as anyone."

"All right," Bolan said. He turned to Yin and handed him the M-16. He demonstrated the safety switch just above the trigger. "This has a 20-round magazine, so don't use it full-auto. It'll recoil out of control for you. The safety is off."

"Why not the AK?" Yin asked.

"Harder to reload quickly for a novice, and I need the shorter length in close quarters," Bolan explained. "The AK kicks harder, and the M-16 is lighter and easier to handle one shot at a time."

Yin took the M-16, then put his finger straight just like he'd observed Bolan doing with the rifle. "Right?" he asked.

"To the shoulder and use the sights when it's time to shoot," Bolan told him. "You'll do fine if it does get bad. I'll do my best to keep them off you."

Bolan slung the AK across his back, then drew his

Walther, affixing a suppressor to the end. "We're not going in guns blazing. Quick and silent in. Quick and silent out."

Arana and Yin both nodded.

"It's getting dark, and the ATVs are relatively quiet. We'll swing around the far side of the perimeter, looking for an unlit corner," Bolan said. "We'll drive to a hundred yards out, park, and Yin and I will go in. Arana, guard the vehicles and cover us if it gets nasty. I'll provide support while Yin gets the kids back to you."

The Executioner took a deep breath. "I'm not going to lie to any of you. This is going to be a serious gamble. Any of us could die for what we are doing here. I will work to take most of the risk myself, but until the facility is destroyed, none of you are safe."

"I've risked my life for the past five days," Arana said. "What's another few hours?"

Yin put his arm around her shoulders. "I can't think of a better way to leave my old life behind."

Grandfather Wangara nodded, smiling, patting the stock of Bolan's VEPR. Nothing more needed to be said by the shaman, his eyes unfocused as he listened to the songs of his ancestors streaming through his consciousness.

Crown scanned the others, then looked at the weapon Bolan had given him. The satellite phone would enable him to crush an international smuggling conspiracy with only a few spoken words. He locked eyes with the Executioner. "I'll make up for looking the other way and endangering my children," he said.

Bolan gave them all a nod of approval. They were ordinary people driven by extraordinary circumstance. They had all made their peace.

Now it was time for them to make war.

LUCENZO AND LAW SPIED upon the base through binoculars. Camouflage netting and a sudden shutdown on the lights made things more difficult. Bobby Yeung had been smart enough to equip his guards with red-filter flashlights. The wavelengths were too weak to show at range as anything more than indistinct ripples of light and shadow.

They had observed the sniper battle that had gone on between the assassin and the poachers, watching as twelve men were devastated by a single man's marksmanship and tactics. It was at once a reminder of their own bloody routs, and a preview of the rest of the evening's conflict. The triad subboss and the lone mercenary remained quiet about the traumatic memories raised by the long-range war, but a single glance expressed their inner thoughts.

All they needed was that solitary warrior to unleash his unique brand of warfare on the odds they were facing. There was no way that one man could survive Yeung's combined force. Even if he did succeed, he wouldn't be ready for a blindside attack by Law's forces. The Black Rose's king of Darwin had twenty grim guns at his back, including his own weapons and the experienced Lucenzo.

"It'll start soon," Lucenzo said finally. "He'll use the cover of darkness. And he won't wait for the guards to tire out until dawn."

"He'll go after them while they're fresh?" Law asked.

"Would you expect trouble immediately?" Lucenzo countered.

"He waited until my first shift was exhausted to strike," Law answered.

"And that's what Yeung will be expecting, too. This man doesn't flatten enemy forces single-handedly by doing what his enemy expects. He outthinks you by knowing how you'd deal with a threat and going for the least expected response," Lucenzo explained. "We'll keep an eye out. We won't hear the first few shots of this round, but soon enough, we'll know it's going on."

"If he's so smart," Law began, "he'd know we're already here."

Lucenzo nodded.

"So he will be expecting us," Law said.

"Your goal is to win back the facility and take it over for yourself," Lucenzo answered. "My goal is to cement my place as the Black Rose's chief executioner. We're going to have to take a calculated risk, and you've got my plan."

Law nodded, filled with dread.

Two hundred yards behind them, Obwe Wangara moved toward the position he had chosen to cover Bolan, Arana and Yin. Though he was in his sixties, he'd lived in the outback long enough to be in great condition. He slid through the shadows slowly but easily, to avoid overtaxing his muscles.

He spotted Law and Lucenzo and their private army and lowered himself to the ground. His ancestors had guided him through the darkness, bringing him to a threat that the crusader had been unaware of.

Wangara took a deep, quiet breath, pumping oxygen into his system and he shouldered his rifle. The old Aboriginal tribesman would provide fire support, just not in the way they'd originally planned.

14

With Yin at his heels, the Executioner crept across the last twenty feet to the facility, his Walther P-99 leading the way. The compound had been cast into darkness, but both Bolan and Yin could see the movements of guards, their red-filter flashlights glowing like demonic eyes in the darkness as they patrolled, looking for the monster coming for them. Bolan turned to Yin and made a hand signal for him to wait, hidden out of sight.

The Black Rose defector nodded. He'd slung his rifle and had improvised a silenced handgun. He'd traded Sheriff Crown his CZ P-01 for a Ruger GP-100 .357 Magnum revolver. By wrapping some heavy tarp around his gun hand, the canvas would capture the hot gases from the revolver, but limit it to being only six shots, less if the superheated Magnum rounds ignited the rags. Yin knew if he couldn't stop a momentary threat with one muffled shot, the mission was doomed anyhow. Gunfire would bring Yeung's guards down on him, cutting off the only escape path for Stone and the hostages he intended to rescue. The thought of dying didn't fill him with fear, but a crushing loneliness and a fear of failure. Yin wouldn't see Arana again, and the children they'd come to save would never see their family again. That kind of loss made death seem like a sweet release.

Fully aware of the consequences of a screwup, he banished all such thoughts to be aware, fully in the moment. Nothing would escape his notice.

Already, though, that was too late because Stone had disappeared like a ghost into the shadows. Yin fought to clear the eeriness of the big man's stealth, concentrating on the bobbing red flares of flashlights and the crunch of footsteps and hushed voices communicating with each other.

Get back soon, Stone, Yin thought, keeping his wrapped Ruger clutched tightly in his fist.

EVEN THOUGH THE BLOCKHOUSE wasn't processing heroin for redistribution, the air was heavy with the stink of the chemicals needed to cut the opium into its most addictive form. Bolan had tied a damp handkerchief around his nose and mouth in order to filter out the stench and to minimize its nauseating effects. He pushed the Walther back into its shoulder holster and drew his fighting blade. A gunshot in this atmosphere, even with a sound suppressor, would increase the risk of an explosion due to the flammable fumes from the chemical cutting agents.

Bolan stalked through the shadowed blockhouse, weaving between storage crates and worktables, cutting his path left or right behind cover when he spotted a flashlight-wielding guard patrolling through the building. He'd been forced to enter the blockhouse on the opposite side of where Crown's children had been held as that was where he and Yin had discovered a small gap in the security of the facility compound. Though the traverse of the long floor had only taken three minutes, it felt like an eternity as he skulked, branching off down paths of least resistance.

The only benefit of the sight of patrolling guards was the fact that he could observe them more carefully. The men inside were wearing filter masks to deal with the choking fumes wafting through the blockhouse. They wore machetes in belt sheaths, guns strapped down firmly in full flap holsters. The armament suggested that should a conflict erupt in the darkened blockhouse, it wouldn't erupt into a blazing fireball that would immolate everyone involved. Still, cries of alarm would be raised, enabling guards outside to settle in to cover the exits, ready to shoot anyone trying to get out.

The sight of filter masks also gave hope to Bolan that he wouldn't be dealing with half-suffocated children on the escape. It was likely that they would be wearing filter masks as well, because mutilated corpses wouldn't hold as much terror as living, tortured kids.

When Bolan found the cage, he could see the faces of Ansen Crown's children, a ten-year-old boy named Sage and an eight year-old girl, Nancy. Their mouths and noses were covered with white filter cups, their blond hair matted to their skulls with cowlicks spiking up here and there on their scalps. Two sets of eyes went wide when they saw him, a towering shape dressed all in black, wielding a dull-finished knife poking out of his fist.

Bolan scanned left and right, looking for Yeung's

guards, but the triad boss had layered his troops into shifts, cutting down on available manpower to secure every foot of the base. In keeping a reserve of gunmen fresh and ready, he'd exposed gaps in his defenses. A knot of barbed wire was wrapped around the chain-link-fence door holding the pair of children inside. Sage's hand was covered with cuts from trying to bend the heavy-gauge spiked wire apart to get to freedom. Nancy had wrapped the worst of the cuts with strips from her red dress.

Bolan sheathed his knife and pulled out a multitool. He flipped it open, exposing the needle-nose pliers and wire cutters within. The scything blades of the wire snips released a tiny singsong as he popped through strands as he squeezed. Loops fell away from the improvised lock, and in a moment, he had the gate open.

"Your father sent me," Bolan whispered to the pair. "Are you all right to walk?"

Both nodded, quiet with fear. The Executioner drew his knife and extended his free hand to Sage. "Hold your sister's hand and don't let go," he whispered.

Bolan led the brother and sister through the darkness. Rather than blindly retracing his steps—to make the most of his time inside the blockhouse—he kept on the alert for holes in the guards' patrol patterns. There was a grunt in the distance behind them, and Bolan's limited Chinese picked up the sudden cry of alarm.

The shout turned Bolan's attention to one side for a mere moment, and when he looked back, he spotted two guards stumbling into view. Bolan let go of the Crown children as the first of the triad pair reached for the machete in his belt. The Gerber's razor-sharp point sank through the man's breastbone in one swift lunge, and the Executioner grabbed the handle of the half-drawn machete as the dying guard's rib cage and heart tugged the fighting knife from his hands.

With a swift movement, Bolan whipped the heavy point of the machete across the center of the second guard's face, caving in one cheekbone. The Chinese gangster gurgled messily as his skull cracked under the savage impact. Bolan cut off the guard's burbling by reversing the blade's point and ripping out his throat. The entire exchange had taken only moments, but two corpses flopping to the ground had drawn the attention of other guards patrolling the blockhouse.

Bolan didn't need to be fluent in Chinese, as the inflection of "Get him!" remained the same in every language. He took Sage's hand and he pulled brother and sister along in a ground-eating trot, his normal swift pace scaled back to accommodate the children. Nancy was quiet to the point of seeming catatonic, and Sage muttered under his mask at the goriness of how completely the Executioner had destroyed two human beings.

Bolan was almost at the door where he'd entered the blockhouse when he spotted motion out of the corner of his eye. He whirled, bringing up the machete with reflexive speed honed by decades of conflict. Steel sparked on steel as a Black Rose machete bounced off Bolan's parry. With no intention of extending the exposure of Sage and Nancy Crown to danger, he let go of the boy's hand and snapped a roundhouse kick into the triad thug's gut, folding him over. The Executioner chopped the stunned mobster in the back of the head with one powerful swing of his machete. The man collapsed to the ground in a tangled mass of arms and legs.

"Go, now," Bolan ordered. The children obeyed, rushing to the door.

The Executioner turned to face down another pair of guards rushing to cut off the escape. One of the men barreled straight at Bolan, while the other swung wide to avoid him and to intercept the children. Bolan lunged toward the threat to the kids, swiping at the guard's shoulder with his machete. The blade stuck in heavy muscle and bone, but the impact smashed the racing guard into the floor face-first, his nose and jaw crushed by a hard collision with the concrete floor. The gangster who had made his move to tackle Bolan recovered from the Executioner's sudden sidestep by somersaulting to his feet, machete whirling in a figure-eight arc.

The Black Rose man smirked at the unarmed man before him. "You die in many cuts, no?"

"No," Bolan answered. With a flash of movement, he whipped one of his improvised throwing knives from its forearm sheath, the sharp paring blade's point seemingly attracted to the blade man's right eye by a magnet. With his orb destroyed, the guard howled in agony, dropping his machete. The Executioner closed range with the disarmed guard, seized him with a hand on his chin and the top of his head, and twisted with every ounce of his strength. The sickening snap of a spine ended the suffering wail from the Black Rose hatchet man, and Bolan discarded the still-standing corpse by throwing him into the path of a third guard who was rushing to join the conflict.

With a lunge, Bolan was outside, sweeping his AK-47

from over his shoulder. Yin was true to his word, not waiting one moment for Bolan when he saw the kids. The young mobster was tearing across the desert toward Arana and the ATVs, carrying Sage and Nancy under his arms as if they were footballs.

A single gunshot cracked in the distance, and a triad sentry who had spotted Yin's mad dash to freedom collapsed with a bullet through his upper chest. In the distance, Arana worked the bolt on her weapon, knowing that her gunshot had just alerted the whole compound.

It was a nonissue. The Crown children were out of danger range. Bolan swung his submachine gun around to sweep the perimeter for more threatening gangsters. With a hammering muzzle-blast, the Executioner chopped down a pair of Black Rose gunmen as they aimed at Arana.

THE GUNFIRE JOLTED Yeung as he tried to take a quick catnap to preserve his alertness for later in the night. He reached for his Glock and kicked out from behind his desk. One of his lieutenants raced in, panic on his face.

"Stone took the sheriff's kids!" Chow shouted over the distant rattle of automatic weapons. "We've got guards moving to surround him, but the punks are nowhere to be seen!"

"Of course not," Yeung snarled. "He's providing a distraction. But who's helping him?"

"The Aborigines?" Chow asked.

"I don't care," Yeung decided. "I want everyone awake and fighting now!"

"With all this racket—" Chow began before he was

interrupted by a ground-shaking blast. The night peeled away to harsh daylight by a rising fireball from the blockhouse.

Without fear of endangering Sage and Nancy Crown, Bolan had taken the opportunity to toss a Soviet stick-grenade into the depths of the blockhouse. The antitank blaster produced enough heat to ignite the fumes. The blast knocked Yeung and Chow to the floor.

"No," Yeung muttered, crawling to the window of his office to look at the burning remains of his warehouse and drug lab. He'd tried to load as much of the product onto the transport planes hidden by the airfield, but the facility had five years' worth of accumulated weapons and drugs. It would have taken five times as many planes as were on the field to rescue even half of what he'd kept in reserve there.

A raging fire tore through the heart of the blockhouse, touching flame to crates full of contraband and black market rifles.

Millions of dollars' worth of product was being reduced to ash by a single grenade, and the vents atop the camouflaged warehouse burst with tongues of orange and yellow seeking open air to burn.

"No," Yeung growled, crushing the grip of his Glock with all of his strength, the harsh checkering of the plastic frame clawing his fingers and palm.

He smashed out the glass of the window with the barrel of his Glock and fired fifteen shots into the night, 9 mm pills spitting through the firelit shadows.

"I'll kill you, Stone!" Yeung bellowed at the top of his lungs, his rage peaking above the roar and pop of the inferno consuming the gold mine he'd set up for himself.

The Black Rose boss kicked the wall under the window and whirled to join his soldiers in fighting back against the Executioner.

OBWE WANGARA JUMPED as the mushroom of flame and debris rocketed through the roof of the blockhouse, the sudden flare of the explosion making him flinch and punch out a .300 Winchester Magnum round that sizzled into the shoulder blade of one of Frankie Law's soldiers, severing his spine and pitching him into the dirt like a rag doll.

"Oh, shit," Wangara grumbled as he saw the triad gunmen on either side of the corpse jump to the side, bringing up their guns. It had been a long time, and he'd allowed his finger to rest on the trigger while scanning the crowd of mobsters all decked out for war. His involuntary reflex had started a fight, and the Aborigine gripped the VEPR tightly, firing as fast as he could. Across the short range between himself and the Chinese gunmen, he was at point-blank for the high-powered cartridges, not having to worry about bullet drop. All he had to do was aim and pull the trigger, the bullets hitting where his scope pointed.

One of Law's gunslingers jerked as he took two .300 Magnum bullets through the chest. The second gunman cut loose with his assault rifle, but in the darkness, and with the flash suppressor on the end of the VEPR's barrel, the gangster was simply shooting at shadows, not knowing where the attack was coming from.

Lucenzo pushed Law to the ground and broke open the breech on his M-203 grenade launcher, stuffing in a 40 mm cartridge. With a swift motion, he clicked the slid-

ing breech shut and looked around the battlefield. A bullet dug into the earth a few inches from Lucenzo's hip, and
another of Law's gunners lay dying nearby.

Lucenzo made an estimate of range and tugged the
trigger on his M-203, arcing the 40 mm shrapnel grenade
high and into the shadows two hundred yards away in a
nearly straight line from the bullet strike. The hell bomb
landed, its eruption rocking Wangara with a powerful
shock wave. Though his head was left reeling from the explosion, the uneven ground had shielded him from a sheet
of flesh-shredding shrapnel.

Wangara crawled, pulling himself away from his position, staying low. The sun-bright fireball faded in the sky,
reducing visibility dramatically, and without firing any
more shots from the VEPR, he wouldn't attract too much
attention. Even so, Law's gunmen ripped out long bursts
from their assault weapons, filling the night with mayhem
in counterpoint to the conflict in the compound itself.

Wangara prayed to his ancestors. He hoped that they
would make up for his failure to protect his granddaughter and her new boyfriend by jumping the gun. As he
looked up into the starry sky draped over him, he realized
that the automatic fire that had ripped at the desert floor
around him had ceased. Clouds of erupted dirt settled
around him, and the sound of human violence dropped
away to a distant rattle.

Law and Lucenzo had betrayed the element of their
surprise with their response to Wangara's flinching first
shot. Yeung's Black Rose defenders focused on their
muzzle-flashes in the distance and cut loose with savage
abandon.

Wangara felt the storm of conflict unleash its cleansing fury onto the triad's violation of his ancestral homelands.

Yin was thirty feet from the ATVs when the sky split with orange flame behind him. For a moment, he wondered if it was a lightning strike, but the thunder that whipped past him was hot and savage, a flame wind that would have singed the hair from the back of his head if he had been any closer to the blockhouse. Sage and Nancy Crown screamed in fear as Bolan's thunderbolt struck the facility hard enough to shake the earth. Arana triggered her Enfield, helping to keep the Chinese gangsters down.

Yin stumbled and dropped to one knee heavily.

"Yin!" Arana called.

"Run," Yin told the children. "Get to the girl with the bikes."

The Crown children looked at the exhausted young Chinese man who had carried them almost to safety. Sage grabbed his forearm, pulling. "No way, mate! Come on!"

"You can do it," Nancy added, her small hands tugging at his other sleeve. "We've got to go."

Yin winced as he struggled to his feet. His left leg felt hot and numb, and he assumed he'd been shot, except that his pants didn't feel wet. As he put his weight on the limb, he nearly crashed to the ground, his thigh exploding in pain as torn muscles no longer had the strength to support him.

"Move it. I'll be all right," Yin told them. "Go."

He rolled onto his back, tugging his M-16. The selector was set to single shot, and he looked for threats when the deep-throated roar of Arana's bolt-action Enfield erupted just above him.

"Laying down on the job?" she asked.

"Tore some muscles," Yin replied. "I'm not going for a walk anytime soon."

Arana grimaced, then threw her Enfield's strap over her shoulder. She stooped and hooked Yin under his armpits. "You wouldn't have messed up your stupid leg if you hadn't gotten all macho."

She pulled, and Yin kicked into the dirt with his right leg. Sage and Nancy Crown tucked themselves in Arana's shadow as they scrambled the last couple of yards toward the ATVs. The Black Rose gunmen were more interested in the giant wraith whipping through their ranks, having forgotten the young woman nipping at their heels with a World War II–era rifle.

Arana surged, pushing Yin onto the saddle of his ATV. "Can you ride this at least?" she asked.

"I'll be fine," Yin answered. His face was pale, his hair matted to his forehead, drenched in sweat.

"Kids, on my quad," Arana ordered. "Keep up, Yin, please."

The ex-gangster nodded with a weak smile. The ATV had an electric start, saving him from the effort of kick-starting the vehicle. He revved the engine and swung in behind Arana as the Crown children clung to her and each other on the crowded double seat of the ATV.

Yin glanced back, watching the blazing facility recede into the distance behind him, offering a silent prayer that the big man who had given him a second chance could carry the day in battle with Bobby Yeung's army of gunmen. He concentrated on the dunes in front of him, escorting Arana and the children to the safety of the Uluru mound caves.

THE EXECUTIONER, alone and free to move, was in full blitz mode. The moment he'd spared to dump a Soviet RG-41 antitank grenade inside the blockhouse had been well spent. The resultant explosion had broken the momentum of Yeung's bodyguards as they swarmed to pen him in. It focused their attention away from Yin, Arana and the kids. Bolan took the remainder of the RG-41's four-second fuse to find cover in the form of a Toyota Land Cruiser parked nearby. The bulk of the vehicle proved to be a sufficient shield against the sheet of pressure, heat and hurtling debris that his senses weren't left reeling.

The Black Rose soldiers, on the other hand, had been caught completely flat-footed, their eyes and ears overwhelmed by thunder and lightning.

Bolan took advantage of the sudden shock they suffered. With the AK-47 on single-shot, he snapped off a half-dozen precision shots. Six Chinese gangsters collapsed and folded into lifeless lumps. As the other guards recovered their senses, they saw their allies destroyed by the Executioner's marksmanship and let out cries of dismay at the carnage.

Bolan knew from hard experience that most of his opponents were bullies at heart, used to having superior numbers and firepower. When faced with his blitzing assault, the bodies of their comrades stacked like cordwood and their headquarters shaken by explosions and fire, their bravado disappeared, replaced by their true natures.

The Executioner exposed the carrion dogs he fought for the cowards they truly were. Robbed of their symbols of strength and power, they were his for the taking.

15

"How did they get behind us?" Frankie Law asked. "And who are they?"

"Probably Stone's people," Lucenzo growled.

Law fumed for a moment, then looked at the column of fire boiling in the distance.

"We don't have time for this kind of bullshit. We have to hit hard, while everyone's off guard," Lucenzo snapped.

"That should have been my payday, and he destroyed it!" Law grumbled.

"So we get him back for costing you. As long as we can save the bulk of the facility, you can fill it up again in no time," Lucenzo told him.

Law raised his rifle and shouted, rallying his remaining soldiers. "Let's take what's ours!"

THE EXECUTIONER'S BATTLE nearly ended right there. Had it not been for an overzealous Black Rose defender leaping on Bolan's back in an effort to drive the point of his machete through the big American's chest, six AK rounds would not have been stopped by the man's torso. In his zeal to kill Bolan, the triad gangster instead saved him from being gunned down. His weight pulled Bolan to one side, drawing him out of the incessant swarm of autofire that punched into Bobby Yeung's faction of gangsters. Four men fell, screaming as they were ripped from crotch to throat by high-powered bullets.

The Executioner wrenched the corpse off his back and grabbed the dead man's rifle. Holding the AK up with one hand, he swung the muzzle around the corner and fired out the entire magazine. Recoil caused the weapon to buck and jump, spraying bullets wildly across the countryside, but it was Bolan's intent to intimidate the charging squad being led by Law and Lucenzo.

One of the renegade triad gangsters rushing to the edge of the compound was stopped forever, his heart chopped in two by a pair of 7.62 mm slugs. The other members of the surging tide scattered, dropping to the dirt to avoid the wild fusillade launched by the Executioner.

Bolan discarded the empty rifle and recharged his own AK-47. Yeung's people were aiming at the newcomers to the conflict, assuming that Bolan was on their side because he'd opened up on the new enemy. Being tucked behind a corner, cast in shadow, helped to keep the facility defenders from identifying their supposed ally until it was too late. The Executioner rewarded them for their assumption with an RG-41 stick-grenade that tumbled into their midst.

The gangsters were confused by the object that landed at their feet. When the fuse ticked off its final second and exploded, the triad gunmen were still none the wiser as they were blown to pieces.

Stunned and lacerated survivors struggled to recover

from the blast, but Bolan's Kalashnikov growled angrily, issuing its 7.62 mm ComBloc death sentences at 600 rounds per minute. Corpses slumped across the compound, giving the Executioner some breathing room to get out of the main point of collision between the rival Black Rose.

Bolan had taken ten steps out of his previous position when Lucenzo's M-4/M-203 grunted, hurling its 40 mm payload of high explosives toward the spot he'd just vacated. Recognizing the sound instinctively, Bolan lowered his head and charged at full speed, racing with abandon to get out of the casualty radius of the explosive. His headlong charge brought him hard into the body of a Black Rose guard, the impact sending them both flying. Stunned by the sudden collision, Bolan tumbled in the dirt, his rifle torn from his hands. An instant later, the artificial thunderclap detonated and shook Bolan. The triad gunman's allies were bowled over by the nearby blast.

As the Executioner dragged himself to his hands and knees, a second 40 mm shell landed, this one spiking the ground near him. His legs snapping out like a bullfrog's, Bolan launched himself away from ground zero, one clawing hand dragging a Black Rose sentry to him as a human shield. The shock wave rattled him, but the Chinese gangster's body absorbed the shrapnel put off by Lucenzo's grenade. The concussion rolled Bolan and his corpse shield for ten feet.

Those triad soldiers not obliterated by Lucenzo's shell opened fire, spraying their assault weapons along the perimeter. The 40 mm tube popped loudly again. The deadly warhead sailed in a lazy arc to land right in the middle of

Yeung's gunmen, the third grenade cracking pulverizing flesh and bone. By this time, Bolan had ditched the shrapnel-perforated cadaver and raced around to flank Lucenzo, thankful for the Russian-made RG-41 grenades.

While egg-style grenades were less bulky and easier to carry, the stick-handled grenades had great advantages. The first was that their warheads could be larger and carry more explosive. The second, more important advantage was that they could be hurled farther as they carried more initial momentum due to a greater leverage on the toss, their top end separating to carry all the energy of the throw. With a powerful, underhanded lob swing, Bolan launched the RG-41 toward the sound of Lucenzo's grenade launcher. The Vietnam-era grenade tumbled end over end before breaking apart, the lightweight wooden handle falling away while the bulky grenade sailed into a knot of Frankie Law's soldiers, landing short of Lucenzo's position. The grenade, designed for punching through tank skins, went off with devastating force.

Lucenzo's grenade launcher fired a moment after Bolan's RG-41 detonated, but the mercenary's round sailed away from Bolan's position, spiraling into the far side of the compound. Bolan's blast had left most of Law's rebel force stunned or dead.

Bolan drew his Walther P-99 and charged into the group, interested in getting hold of the mercenary's high-firepower weapon and ammunition. He'd long since lost track of his rifle, and if he was going to take care of the rest of Yeung's defensive forces and the aircraft he heard warming up on the airfield, he knew he needed that grenade launcher.

A wounded Chinese gunman lifted a Makarov toward

Bolan, but the Executioner put a 9 mm pill into his mouth to end his suffering. A hand lashed out, grabbing at Bolan's ankle, but it didn't have the strength to hold on, shredded fingers popping open as Bolan continued his charge.

Lucenzo rose shakily to his feet, pulling a Beretta from his waistband. The M-4/M-203 was nowhere to be seen, but the Executioner snapped up his Walther, pouring out silenced bullets as fast as he could work the trigger. Lucenzo jerked, but he was wearing body armor that robbed the relatively low-velocity 9 mm bullets of their power. Lucenzo's Beretta snapped and cracked as the mercenary tried to gun down Bolan. With a lunge, the Executioner threw himself the final few feet, bowling Lucenzo over with a shoulder block.

The two men tumbled to the ground, separating. Bolan had to pivot to face Lucenzo again, and that extra moment of delay exposed him just long enough for Lucenzo to lash out with a fighting knife. Bolan deflected the lethal slash with the frame of his pistol, but the impact jarred the weapon from numbed fingers. He countered by spearing his fingertips at Lucenzo's eyes, only grazing them as the mercenary whipped his head around to escape blindness.

The point of Lucenzo's knife speared up, its razor sharpness carving open Bolan's shirt, barely scratching his skin. Bolan was able to step back, bringing up his knee to jar the mercenary's triceps. Bringing down his elbow, the Executioner snapped Lucenzo's arm, forcing the combat blade to tumble into the dirt. Bolan grabbed a handful of his adversary's leather jacket and wrenched the mercenary up and into a pile-driving fist that crushed the would-be assassin's nose.

Eyes blurred and unfocused, Lucenzo reached up, trying to claw out Bolan's eyes as a last line of defense, but Bolan brought his fist down again, knuckles collapsing Lucenzo's windpipe with a lethal punch. Suddenly suffocating, the mercenary wrenched himself halfway out of his jacket, trying to run off to escape his imminent demise. The Executioner was no longer in the mood to hand out second chances, however, and with a hard whip of his arm, used Lucenzo's jacket like a leash, yanking the mercenary back into range for a spearing side kick that caught him at the base of his skull.

The lifeless man poured into a puddle at Bolan's feet, and the warrior looked around for the prize he'd sought. He saw the black frame of the grenade launcher poking out of some scrubs and took a step toward it. Bolan jerked to a halt and ducked, a gleaming ribbon of steel slicing through the air where his head had been a moment before.

With a somersault, Bolan dived for cover as the whistle of steel through air sounded again, the tip of the flailing blade barely missing Bolan's lower spine. He came up in a crouch, seeing Frankie Law, mirrored silver camp ax in hand, ducking out of sight, disappearing into shadows and smoke before he could draw a knife or recover a firearm to press the battle.

Bolan turned and looked at the nearby M-4 and saw that it had been ruptured, badly bent by the impact of the powerful explosion. The splintered tube of the grenade launcher lay off to the side. The weapon was useless. Bolan raced back to Lucenzo's body, stripping the Beretta magazines from his waistband, then scooping up the 9 mm pistol. He scanned around and found an AK-74 with a folding stock. He dumped the magazine and saw that it was a 5.45 mm design, not compatible with the ammunition he had in his bandolier. He spent a few moments getting more banana clips for the new rifle, dumping his old magazines.

"Better than nothing," he said. He looked around.

Yeung's forces had split their attention between putting out the fires raging through the blockhouse and securing the perimeter. Just to keep them on their toes, the Executioner pulled his last RG-41 antitank grenade and threw it toward a knot of triad gunmen who were dragging crates of AK-105 assault rifles, the arsenal that had been bought from a Russian general selling off his nation's defenses. The antitank grenade detonated in the middle of the Russian rifles and went off. Splintered wood, twisted plastic and mangled steel were pushed out on a wave of concussive force, shattered barrels launched at the speed of arrows, spearing through Chinese torsos without slowing. Pulped corpses bounced in bloody splatters against the ground as the explosion pushed them away from ground zero. Though he hadn't been able to get hold of a rifle with a grenade launcher, a vintage grenade had turned a stockpile of modern assault rifles into a lethal antipersonnel bomb.

Yeung's guard force reacted to the new detonation, spotting the Executioner as he wanted them to. Bolan dived for cover an instant before the surprised Chinese toughs opened fire, their rifles spitting wildly and hitting everything except the lone warrior. Bolan could hear the

Black Rose defenders shouting into radios, calling in their sighting and trying to pen him in. The calls for backup were aimed at giving away his position as they'd last seen it. In order to get the Black Rose hatchet men to where he wanted them to go, he charged across an area of open ground, making certain his hunters saw him racing toward the airplanes warming up on the tarmac.

Though Bolan didn't have a radio to monitor their communications, nor the fluency in Cantonese or Mandarin to make out the nuances of their urgent messages even if he did have access to a walkie-talkie, he did see gunmen shouting into handsets. Bolan slowed as soon as he'd ducked out of their line of sight, checked behind him to see how much he was exposed, then dropped prone, using the corner he'd rounded as concealment.

Five of Yeung's riflemen raced headlong, and when they were ten yards away, Bolan triggered his AK-74. The 5.45 mm slugs speared through shins and knees, knocking the racing gunners onto their stomachs. A second sweep of fire on full-auto raked the Chinese sentries from this life into the next. Bolan snapped out the partially spent magazine and rocked another one home as a second wave of men rushed behind their fallen comrades. The Black Rose Triad gangsters were in a panic. They cut loose with their rifles from the hip, firing wildly.

Flat on the ground, the only things striking Bolan were splinters and shards dislodged as the triad gunners' supersonic bullets chewed through the corner of the wall he was positioned behind. He swept the front sight across the leader of the second wave of attackers and milked a short burst into the gunman's chest, ripping it open and bowling him back into one of his partners. The pair's collision upset the momentum of the racing group of fighters, spreading out their formation to make them easier for Bolan to target. In a grisly game of follow the bouncing ball, Bolan pulled the trigger every time the glowing tritium front sight of his AK intersected a Chinese gunman. In bursts of two and three shots, he ripped apart the remaining trio of gangsters.

The sole survivor of the group threw his rifle and radio away, screaming a surrender as he crawled on his hands and knees away from the death trap the Executioner had set up for him. Bolan dismissed the man, knowing a broken opponent when he saw one. He got to his feet and raced back the way he'd come, pausing only to scoop up the discarded walkie-talkie to bolster his intelligence.

Amid the chaos Bolan heard an irritated cry from toward the airstrip. "Where is he? He hasn't shown up yet! Report!"

That report wouldn't come anytime soon for the defenders of the airfield. Bolan swung around. It wasn't much of a detour, but coming at them from the wrong angle gave the Executioner all the advantage he needed. His AK spoke, cutting a man in two and crushing the skull of a second Black Rose gunman in a devastating opening volley. The Chinese toughs exploded in cries of rage and confusion as Bolan hammered their exposed flank.

With the warning given by their allies, the Black Rose fighters had situated themselves behind cover facing Bolan's expected avenue of approach. Unfortunately for the dug-in guards, that cover provided little protection from the Executioner as he hammered down on them.

The chattering AK ran dry, and Bolan let it drop on its sling, slipping out the Beretta in one swift movement. Drawing the 9 mm pistol was faster than wrestling with the magazine of the Kalashnikov, and it would reload more quickly than the rifle. As the range was only twenty feet by the time his assault rifle had run out of ammo, the handgun was not handicapped by distance.

Bolan popped a Beretta round through the face of one of the sentries who had the reflexes and wits to turn and point his rifle in the direction of the sudden onslaught. Dying reflex jerked the shooter's whole body back, finger tensing on the trigger. The wild burst emptied at contact range into the small of his partner's back.

A third guard opened fire, the muzzle-blast so close to Bolan that he could feel the heat. The barrel was hot as he pushed it aside, sweeping the Beretta below the rifleman's sternum, triggering two shots that plowed into his heart. With his blood pressure rapidly dropping, the gunman collapsed limply over Bolan's arm to form a human shield and soaked up an initial burst from a pair of guards who refused to give up.

The close-range rifle shots started to burst through Bolan's shield, but by the time they exited the corpse, he had thrown himself into a shoulder roll. The sideways dodge gave him enough of a respite to rise to one knee and burn off six shots in rapid fire, peppering the coordinated team before they could adjust their aim. The half-dozen 9 mm bullets ripped through the duo, dumping them into a heap of tangled limbs.

Bolan scooped up an unfired rifle and took aim at a crew of gunmen racing across the tarmac, drawn by the sound of conflict. Flicking the AK to single-shot, he pumped rounds into each charging shadow. He sidestepped with each third pull of the trigger, crab-walking along as he fired on the rest of the guards around the airfield, discarding the partially empty rifle to pick up another. The chatter on the radio he'd clipped to the collar of his shirt had died away. He'd either inflicted heavier losses on the opposition, or they'd gotten wise and moved to another channel.

Bolan visually swept the tarmac first, looking for opposition, then pressed the scan button on the walkie-talkie. There was nothing coming in on any of the handset's programmed frequencies that would have caused the radio to stop and focus on the snippets of conversation. The Executioner tried to measure the losses inflicted on the Black Rose's defensive force.

Before he could fully take stock, a transport plane rolled onto the tarmac, its engines rising in pitch to signify that it was ready for takeoff. The Executioner wrenched the magazine from his rifle and charged toward the aircraft. Yeung had been loading the planes to get them out of Bolan's path of destruction, meaning that the transport was fat, heavily laden with illicit contraband. Bolan rocked a fresh magazine into his weapon as he skidded to a halt in the path of the taxiing aircraft. He shouldered the rifle and opened fire, focusing a stream of high-velocity slugs at the cockpit. He realized that the 5.45 mm bullets wouldn't have the mass to do damage to the heavy-duty turbines that would lift the multiton aircraft. All he could do was hose down the cockpit and hope that the rifle rounds struck the pilot and co-pilot, leaving the plane out of control.

The sound of the transport plane's engines rose to an earsplitting roar, and it shot forward. Bolan held down the trigger, burning off the entire magazine as the aircraft accelerated toward him, its front landing gear aimed right at him, ready to grind him into the tarmac.

The plane's front gear rose, the wheels slicing the air inches over Bolan's head, forcing him to throw himself flat to the ground. He grimaced, realizing that he'd failed in preventing the escape of several tons of heroin and assault rifles from the facility. He glanced toward the retreating aircraft, dreading the potential lives lost because he couldn't bring down the airplane.

Suddenly it lurched violently in flight, one wing rising dramatically, the other dipping down, spearing the runway. The wingtip splintered, aluminum rupturing and hurling off panels in a spray of blazing sparks. The nose whipped down and ground into the tarmac, throwing the plane into a spiraling cartwheel, ripping off the opposite wing and tail boom, hurling them into the scrub at the side of the runway. The fuselage crumpled, splitting in several places as it tumbled out of control before skidding to a halt in a mass of burning metal. With the airstrip littered with a half-dozen massive chunks of wing and tail, the space reserved for takeoff had been cut dramatically, but the Executioner couldn't rely on that to prevent further escape attempts.

Bolan ripped the empty magazine from his AK and found that he'd used up all of his ammunition in frantic combat. He let the rifle hang on its sling and pulled out his Beretta, charging as another plane taxied onto the runway.

16

Bobby Yeung watched as fifty million dollars' worth of heroin and assault rifles were reduced to shrapnel and free-floating fireflies of blazing debris. He squeezed the grip of his Glock, sneering in apoplectic rage. A small jet, laden with Russian automatic weapons, taxied out onto the tarmac. The lone maniac charged at it, still intent on grinding down every ounce of Yeung's work. He realized he no longer had the force left to bring down this one-man army who had smothered his hopes and dreams.

A strangled death cry split the air behind him and Yeung whirled, Glock in hand.

Frankie Law, with a gleaming stainless-steel camp ax drenched in blood, stood over the corpse of two of his guards, his face a mask of hate-filled madness.

"Now we do this the old way, the way the triads did it," Law growled.

Yeung looked back toward the jet as it accelerated in an effort to escape not only gravity, but the humanoid representation of a force of nature that had steam rolled over the facility. "Wait, Frankie. You want Australia?" Yeung said in desperation.

"Want it? It's always been mine, Bobby," Law returned.

Yeung nodded, smiling back at him. "Fine. I don't want the facility. I never did. I hate Australia. I was ordered to come down here. I want to be back in Hong Kong."

"I'll mail you there in little pieces, then," Law cackled.

"We can save what's left of the facility, and our bosses back in China will have no problem with you being in charge. You don't have to take anything by force!" Yeung shouted.

Law stepped forward, eyes betraying a feral wild spirit that had lost touch with its humanity. Yeung knew he didn't have time to find a common ground with the snarling beast before him, and the pistol at his side would be no more effective against him than words. Yeung had seen too many friends armed with guns defeated by foes armed with axes and knives.

Law lunged, and Yeung leaped, diving under his personal jet. He heard the whistle of the camp ax as it parted air instead of his flesh, the lashing strike missing only by inches. Yeung scrambled under the wing of the plane, yelling at the top of his lungs.

"Stone! Stone! Law's in here!"

Law snapped upright, looking out the hangar door, seeing Stone turn from the jet that spewed smoke and flames out of one engine.

"Catch you later, Bobby," Law sang. "I've got bigger prey to bring down."

Yeung sucked down breath to replenish the strength sapped by his sudden panic. He offered up a silent prayer of thanks to his ancestors that his last-ditch ploy of pitting one killing machine against another had worked. He looked to the back entrance of the hangar and made his choice.

Flight was his only option, and it wasn't going to happen in an aircraft. Putting one foot in front of the other, he charged toward the rear exit in a mad run. If he had to jog halfway across the continent back to the coast, it would be a small price to pay for survival. And if he died in the desert, it was at least preferable to being killed by inches at the hands of an ax-wielding maniac.

BOLAN DIDN'T HAVE ANYTHING else to use as an antiaircraft weapon, and the Beretta's bullets wouldn't penetrate the skin of the jet, but he knew he had one tool left at his disposal. Though the AK was empty, it was still far from useless. Without ammunition, it was still handy as one of the simplest weapons around. He sliced away the sling with his knife, snapped out the folding bayonet and cocked his arm behind him.

From rifle to spear, the transformation was completed as the Executioner launched it with every ounce of his strength. The wide turbine mouth of the left engine was Bolan's target, and the rifle sailed the thirty yards into it. Spinning ceramic blades were shattered by the nine-pound weight of the assault rifle, its bulk jammed into the engine and causing a blazing flameout. The jet whirled, its starboard engine still shoving the aircraft at full power, the unbalanced thrust jamming the plane into a ditch off to the side of the airstrip.

The front landing gear snapped, and the nose plunged

into soft earth, the damaged engine pouring out thick, blinding smoke lit orange with the flames from one engine. The starboard engine overheated as the pilot had revved the thrusters in an effort to avoid the wreckage of the first aircraft on the runway. The starboard turbine burned out, flames licking off of it as well.

Over the crackle and roar of dying, burning engines, a cry penetrated his consciousness.

"Stone! Stone! Law's in here!"

He turned, seeing the hangar and Frankie Law, wielding a bloody ax. On the other side of the small plane, Yeung cowered. Law turned to say something to the facility commander, then started toward Bolan.

The Executioner checked the load in his Beretta and saw that he didn't have much ammunition left for the handgun. He holstered the weapon, preferring to conserve his ammunition, and drew the knife he'd bought in Darwin, regretting the loss of the Gerber bowie in the blockhouse. The battle had been intense so far, and even through the heady, painkilling rush of adrenaline, he was beginning to feel fatigue creep into his limbs. The trail of corpses threading from Hong Kong to Darwin through Alice Springs and finally to the shadow of Ayers Rock had been long and bloody, but it wasn't over.

Bolan flipped the knife into an ice-pick grip, the heavy spine of the blade against his forearm as a means of protection, though he didn't want to pretend that it would stop the relentless stroke of an ax. Rather than drop into a defensive stance, he charged to meet Law partway, not in compromise but in brutal conflict. Law howled and let fly with the camp ax.

The ring of crashing metal filled the air. Law's swing took him off balance, but the Executioner was braced and prepared for the impact. He whirled, driving a hard fist into the kidney of the Chinese gangster. Law's empty hand whipped out, hard knuckles lashing across Bolan's jaw, jarring him, knocking him to one knee.

Law snarled. He swung the hatchet in an uppercut, and Bolan had to somersault to avoid the wicked slash. Law wailed in frustration that after three swings, he still had not drawn the Executioner's blood. He chopped down, but Bolan kicked up, his foot striking Law's forearm and stopping the ax blade's downward momentum. Maniacal power was the only thing that kept the handle clamped in Law's grasp. Bolan stabbed out with his other foot, thumping Law in the chest and pushing him backward.

Bolan was on all fours, moving to get to his feet when Law speared into him, the flat of the ax swatting him across the side of his head. The rampaging Chinese gangster would have ended the fight right there had he still the focus to aim the blade at a spot just above Bolan's ear, but the broadside of the blade slapped instead, dazing instead of crushing skull. Bolan wrenched his knife up into Law's gut, the point spearing through his soft viscera, lodging deep into intestines.

Law noticed the fatal stab wound, but his reaction was anything but surrender and collapse. A rocketing fist staggered Bolan onto his back, the knife handle slipping from the big American's fingers. The gangster bellowed and swung his ax again.

Bolan lunged for the knife handle sticking out of Law's

gut. He pushed on the handle, twisting it violently. Law's fist cracked across Bolan's jaw, bouncing his head on the runway, despite the fact that he'd opened a huge gash through Law's belly.

Bolan felt the knife come loose into his hand as Law stepped back, dropping his ax on the tarmac.

"You fought well," Law rasped. "Too bad you're on the wrong side. You'd have been more useful than Lucenzo."

Finally, the dying man's strength left him, limbs falling limply to the concrete.

Panting, Bolan knelt by the corpse of the Black Rose gangster for several long moments. The battle was over.

"STONE!" A GIRL'S VOICE called. "Stone!"

Arana Wangara came running up, the Enfield in her hands.

"Where's Yin and the kids?" Bolan asked, his words weighed down by adrenaline crash.

"They're fine. They're with Grandfather. He took a pounding from a nearby grenade explosion, but aside from being knocked silly, he looks like he's all right," she explained. "What about you?"

Bolan accepted her support as he staggered to his feet, feeling the pounding he'd taken deep in his bones. "I've had better days. But there's still work to do. I need to borrow that rifle."

The young woman looked at the hangar. Chinese aircrews were abandoning their aircraft in droves, racing out into the desert. She handed him the Enfield. "Those planes aren't going anywhere," she said.

Bolan drew a bead on an aviation fuel tank inside the hangar where the four remaining planes idled, engines whining. "I'm making sure none of this contraband goes anywhere."

He pulled the trigger and the Enfield barked. Jet fuel squirted in a ten-foot stream, spreading in a puddle around the wheels of one jet. Bolan ricocheted a second round off the concrete, the spark of the copper-jacketed slug on stone turning the growing lake of fuel into a rising inferno. The private jet parked on top of the puddle bounced, wings bending upward under the superheated air pressure rocketing toward the roof. The fuel in the wings ignited, the aluminum shells ballooning with internal explosions that snapped the jet in two.

Spreading flames and shrapnel sprayed onto the other aircraft, a chain reaction of devastation that blazed through the hangar, reducing it to a fire pit.

"You don't mess around," Arana said.

Bolan looked at the teenager and smiled weakly. "All in a day's work. I just wish I knew where Yeung was."

"I saw someone making a beeline straight north. In the dark, I couldn't be sure, but it looked like he was wearing the same suit Yeung was," Arana told him. "The ATV's back there."

Bolan slung the Enfield over his shoulder, and as an afterthought, he picked up Frankie Law's camp ax. Arana eyed the chopped, bloody edge.

"What are you going to do with that?" she asked.

The Executioner felt the weight of the hatchet. "Take care of business the old-fashioned way."

Bolan and Arana headed off toward the ATV, ready to end this night of carnage.

BOBBY YEUNG HAD RUN OUT of steam by the time he'd raced full out for fifteen minutes. His legs felt like soggy noodles, his chest burning as he tried to breathe fast enough to replenish the oxygen in his lungs. The dry air made each breath feel as if he were dragging a coarse towel through his mouth, his sweat-soaked hair draped over his eyes.

He dropped to his knees and vomited, emptying the contents of his stomach onto the ground in front of him.

Yeung glanced back and saw the headlights of an ATV bouncing after him, and his heart sank. He looked at the small Glock in his hand and realized that whatever he did, he was a dead man. He hurled the pistol away.

The headlights grew in size, and the ATV came to a halt not far from him.

"Yeung," Bolan's voice called.

"Stone," Yeung said, defeated.

Bolan threw the ax, the blade sinking into the dirt between Yeung's knees.

Yeung looked at the hatchet poking out of the ground, then up to the man who had destroyed everything he'd worked for. He knew there was no hope for his return to Hong Kong.

"You win," Yeung said. "But I want to make a deal. I'll help you hand the triad over to the authorities."

Bolan nodded. "I'm listening," he said.

"I'm sick of all of this shit," Yeung moaned. "You want all the information you need to take my bosses out, you've got it. I'm offering up my triad to save my skin."

Epilogue

"Good work, Striker," Barbara Price said. "The Black Rose Triad has pulled out of Australia completely."

Mack Bolan stood in the bright sunshine outside the Sydney airport. "I'm heading to Hong Kong, Barb," he said. "I've got one more loose end to tie up."

"Eugene Waylon won't be causing any more trouble," Price said.

"What's happened?" the Executioner asked.

"It seems Bobby Yeung sent word to his bosses before you captured him. He tried to blame Waylon for sending someone named Stone to take them all down so he could take over the drug-processing facility himself. The triad took care of him before we could pick him up." Price sighed. "You've done all you can there," she said. "Unfortunately there's another situation that needs your attention."

Bolan took a deep breath. "I'm on my way."